‘She bared her poor curst arm . . .’

THOMAS HARDY

The Withered Arm

Contents

The Withered Arm

I
A LORN MILKMAID

It was an eighty-cow dairy, and the troop of milkers, regular and supernumerary, were all at work; for, though the time of year was as yet but early April, the feed lay entirely in water-meadows and the cows were 'in full pail'. The hour was about six in the evening, and three-fourths of the large, red, rectangular animals having been finished off, there was opportunity for a little conversation.

'He brings home his bride tomorrow, I hear. They've come as far as Anglebury today.'

The voice seemed to proceed from the belly of the cow called Cherry, but the speaker was a milking-woman, whose face was buried in the flank of that motionless beast.

'Has anybody seen her?' said another.

There was a negative response from the first. 'Though they say she's a rosy-cheeked, tisty-tosty little body enough,' she added; and as the milkmaid spoke she turned her face so that she could glance past her cow's tail to the other side of the barton, where a thin, faded woman of thirty milked somewhat apart from the rest.

'Years younger than he, they say,' continued the second, with also a glance of reflectiveness in the same direction.

'How old do you call him, then?'

'Thirty or so.'

'More like forty,' broke in an old milkman near, in a long white pinafore or 'wropper', and with the brim of his hat tied down, so that he looked like a woman. ''A was born before our Great Weir was builded, and I hadn't man's wages when I laved water there.'

The discussion waxed so warm that the purr of the milk-streams became jerky, till a voice from another cow's belly cried with authority, 'Now then, what the Turk do it matter to us about Farmer Lodge's age, or Farmer Lodge's new mis'ess? I shall have to pay him nine pound a year for the rent of every one of these milchers, whatever his age or hers. Get on with your work, or 'twill be dark before we have done. The evening is pinking in a'ready.' This speaker was the dairyman himself, by whom the milkmaids and men were employed.

Nothing more was said publicly about Farmer Lodge's wedding, but the first woman murmured under her cow to her next neighbour, ''Tis hard for *she*,' signifying the thin worn milkmaid aforesaid.

'Oh no,' said the second. 'He hasn't spoken to Rhoda Brook for years.'

When the milking was done they washed their pails and hung them on a many-forked stand made of the peeled limb of an oak-tree, set upright in the earth, and resembling a colossal antlered horn. The majority then dispersed in various directions homeward. The thin woman who had not spoken was joined by a boy of twelve or thereabout, and the twain went away up the field also.

Their course lay apart from that of the others, to a lonely spot high above the water-meads, and not far from the border of Egdon Heath, whose dark countenance was visible in the distance as they drew nigh to their home.

'They've just been saying down in barton that your father brings his young wife home from Anglebury tomorrow,' the woman observed. 'I shall want to send you for a few things to market, and you'll be pretty sure to meet 'em.'

'Yes, mother,' said the boy. 'Is father married, then?'

'Yes . . . You can give her a look, and tell me what she's like, if you do see her.'

'Yes, mother.'

'If she's dark or fair, and if she's tall – as tall as I. And if she seems like a woman who has ever worked for a living, or one that has been always well off, and has never done anything, and shows marks of the lady on her, as I expect she do.'

'Yes.'

They crept up the hill in the twilight, and entered the cottage. It was thatched, and built of mud-walls, the surface of which had been washed by many rains into channels and depressions that left none of the original flat face visible; while here and there a rafter showed like a bone protruding through the skin.

She was kneeling down in the chimney-corner, before two pieces of turf laid together with the heather inwards, blowing at the red-hot ashes with her breath till the turves flamed. The radiance lit her pale cheek, and made her dark eyes, that had once been handsome, seem handsome anew. 'Yes,' she resumed, 'see if she is dark or fair, and if you can, notice if her hands are white; if not, see if they look as though she had ever done housework, or are milker's hands like mine.'

The boy again promised, inattentively this time, his mother not observing that he was cutting a notch with his pocket-knife in the beech-backed chair.

II
THE YOUNG WIFE

The road from Anglebury to Holmstoke is in general level; but there is one place where a sharp ascent breaks its monotony. Farmers homeward-bound from the former market-town, who trot all the rest of the way, walk their horses up this short incline.

The next evening, while the sun was yet bright, a handsome new gig, with a lemon-coloured body and red wheels, was spinning westward along the level highway at the heels of a powerful mare. The driver was a yeoman in the prime of life, cleanly shaven like an actor, his face being toned to that bluish-vermilion hue which so often graces a thriving farmer's features when returning home after successful dealings in the town. Beside him sat a woman, many years his junior – almost, indeed, a girl. Her face too was fresh in colour, but it was of a totally different quality – soft and evanescent, like the light under a heap of rose-petals.

Few people travelled this way, for it was not a turnpike-road; and the long white riband of gravel that stretched before them was empty, save of one small scarce-moving speck, which presently resolved itself into the figure of a boy, who was creeping on at a snail's pace, and continually looking behind him – the heavy bundle he carried being some excuse for, if not the reason of, his dilatoriness. When the bouncing gig-party slowed at the bottom of the incline above mentioned, the pedestrian was only a few yards in front. Supporting the large bundle by putting one hand on his hip, he turned and looked straight at the farmer's wife as though he would read her through and through, pacing along abreast of the horse.

The low sun was full in her face, rendering every feature, shade, and contour distinct, from the curve of her little nostril to the colour of her eyes. The farmer, though he seemed annoyed at the boy's persistent presence, did not order him to get out of the way; and thus the lad preceded them, his hard gaze never leaving her, till they reached the top of the ascent, when the farmer trotted on with relief in his lineaments – having taken no outward notice of the boy whatever.

'How that poor lad stared at me!' said the young wife.

'Yes, dear; I saw that he did.'

'He is one of the village, I suppose?'

'One of the neighbourhood. I think he lives with his mother a mile or two off.'

'He knows who we are, no doubt?'

'Oh yes. You must expect to be stared at just at first, my pretty Gertrude.'

'I do, – though I think the poor boy may have looked at us in the hope we might relieve him of his heavy load, rather than from curiosity.'

'Oh no,' said her husband off-handedly. 'These country lads will carry a hundredweight once they get it on their backs; besides, his pack had more size than weight in it. Now, then, another mile and I shall be able to show you our house in the distance – if it is not too dark before we get there.' The wheels spun round, and particles flew from their periphery as before, till a white house of ample dimensions revealed itself, with farm-buildings and ricks at the back.

Meanwhile the boy had quickened his pace, and turning up a by-lane some mile and half short of the white farmstead, ascended towards the leaner pastures, and so on to the cottage of his mother.

She had reached home after her day's milking at the outlying dairy, and was washing cabbage at the doorway in the declining light. 'Hold up the net a moment,' she said, without preface, as the boy came up.

He flung down his bundle, held the edge of the cabbage-net, and as she filled its meshes with the dripping leaves she went on, 'Well, did you see her?'

'Yes; quite plain.'

'Is she ladylike?'

'Yes; and more. A lady complete.'

'Is she young?'

'Well, she's growed up, and her ways are quite a woman's.'

'Of course. What colour is her hair and face?'

'Her hair is lightish, and her face as comely as a live doll's.'

'Her eyes, then, are not dark like mine?'

'No – of a bluish turn, and her mouth is very nice and red; and when she smiles, her teeth show white.'

'Is she tall?' said the woman sharply.

'I couldn't see. She was sitting down.'

'Then do you go to Holmstoke church tomorrow morning: she's sure to be there. Go early and notice her walking in, and come home and tell me if she's taller than I.'

'Very well, mother. But why don't you go and see for yourself?'

'*I* go to see her! I wouldn't look up at her if she were to pass my window this instant. She was with Mr Lodge, of course. What did he say or do?'

'Just the same as usual.'

'Took no notice of you?'

'None.'

Next day the mother put a clean shirt on the boy, and started him off for Holmstoke church. He reached the ancient little pile when the door was just being opened, and he was the first to enter. Taking his seat by the font, he watched all the parishioners file in. The well-to-do Farmer Lodge came nearly last; and his young wife, who accompanied him, walked up the aisle with the shyness natural to a modest woman who had appeared thus for the first time. As all other eyes were fixed upon her, the youth's stare was not noticed now.

When he reached home his mother said 'Well?' before he had entered the room.

'She is not tall. She is rather short,' he replied.

'Ah!' said his mother, with satisfaction.

'But she's very pretty – very. In fact, she's lovely.' The youthful freshness of the yeoman's wife had evidently made an impression even on the somewhat hard nature of the boy.

'That's all I want to hear,' said his mother quickly. 'Now, spread the table-cloth. The hare you caught is very tender; but mind that nobody catches you. – You've never told me what sort of hands she had.'

'I have never seen 'em. She never took off her gloves.'

'What did she wear this morning?'

'A white bonnet and a silver-coloured gownd. It whewed and whistled so loud when it rubbed against the pews that the lady coloured up more than ever for very shame at the noise, and pulled it in to keep it from touching; but when she pushed into her seat, it whewed more than ever. Mr Lodge, he seemed pleased, and his waistcoat stuck out, and his great golden seals hung like a lord's; but she seemed to wish her noisy gownd anywhere but on her.'

'Not she! However, that will do now.'

These descriptions of the newly-married couple were continued from time to time by the boy at his mother's request, after any chance encounter he had had with them. But Rhoda Brook, though she might easily have seen young Mrs Lodge for herself by walking a couple of miles, would never attempt an excursion towards the quarter where the farmhouse lay. Neither did she, at the daily milking in the dairyman's yard on Lodge's outlying second farm, ever speak on the subject of the recent marriage. The dairyman, who rented the cows of Lodge, and knew perfectly the tall milkmaid's history, with manly kindliness always kept the gossip in the cow-barton from annoying Rhoda. But the atmosphere thereabout was full of the subject during the first days of Mrs Lodge's arrival; and from her boy's description and the casual words of the other milkers, Rhoda Brook could raise a mental image of the unconscious Mrs Lodge that was realistic as a photograph.

III
A VISION

One night, two or three weeks after the bridal return, when the boy was gone to bed, Rhoda sat a long time over the turf ashes that she had raked out in front of her to extinguish them. She contemplated so intently the new wife, as presented to her in her mind's eye over the embers, that she forgot the lapse of time. At last, wearied with her day's work, she too retired.

But the figure which had occupied her so much during this and the previous days was not to be banished at night. For the first time Gertrude Lodge visited the supplanted woman in her dreams. Rhoda Brook dreamed – since her assertion that she really saw, before falling asleep, was not to be believed – that the young wife, in the pale silk dress and white bonnet, but with features shockingly distorted, and wrinkled as by age, was sitting upon her chest as she lay. The pressure of Mrs Lodge's person grew heavier; the blue eyes peered cruelly into her face; and then the figure thrust forward its left hand mockingly, so as to make the wedding-ring it wore glitter in Rhoda's eyes. Maddened mentally, and nearly suffocated by pressure, the sleeper struggled; the incubus, still regarding her, withdrew to the foot of the bed, only, however, to come forward by degrees, resume her seat, and flash her left hand as before.

Gasping for breath, Rhoda, in a last desperate effort, swung out her right hand, seized the confronting spectre by its obtrusive left arm, and whirled it backward to the floor, starting up herself as she did so with a low cry.

'Oh, merciful heaven!' she cried, sitting on the edge of the bed in a cold sweat, 'that was not a dream – she was here!'

She could feel her antagonist's arm within her grasp even now – the very flesh and bone of it, as it seemed. She looked on the floor whither she had whirled the spectre, but there was nothing to be seen.

Rhoda Brook slept no more that night, and when she went milking at the next dawn they noticed how pale and haggard she looked. The milk that she drew quivered into the pail; her hand had not calmed even yet, and still retained the feel of the arm. She came home to breakfast as wearily as if it had been supper-time.

'What was that noise in your chimmer, mother, last night?' said her son. 'You fell off the bed, surely?'

'Did you hear anything fall? At what time?'

'Just when the clock struck two.'

She could not explain, and when the meal was done went silently about her household work, the boy assisting her, for he hated going afield on the farms, and she indulged his reluctance. Between eleven and twelve the garden-gate clicked, and she lifted her eyes to the window. At the bottom of the garden, within the gate, stood the woman of her vision. Rhoda seemed transfixed.

'Ah, she said she would come!' exclaimed the boy, also observing her.

'Said so – when? How does she know us?'

'I have seen and spoken to her. I talked to her yesterday.'

'I told you,' said the mother, flushing indignantly, 'never to speak to anybody in that house, or go near the place.'

'I did not speak to her till she spoke to me. And I did not go near the place. I met her in the road.'

'What did you tell her?'

'Nothing. She said, "Are you the poor boy who had to bring the heavy load from market?" And she looked at my boots, and said they would not keep my feet dry if it came on wet, because they were so cracked. I told her I lived with my mother, and we had enough to do to keep ourselves, and that's how it was; and she said then, "I'll come and bring you some better boots, and see your mother." She gives away things to other folks in the meads besides us.'

Mrs Lodge was by this time close to the door – not in her silk, as Rhoda had seen her in the bed-chamber, but in a morning hat, and gown of common light material, which became her better than silk. On her arm she carried a basket.

The impression remaining from the night's experience was still strong. Brook had almost expected to see the wrinkles, the scorn, and the cruelty on her visitor's face. She would have escaped an interview, had escape been possible. There was, however, no back-door to the cottage, and in an instant the boy had lifted the latch to Mrs Lodge's gentle knock.

'I see I have come to the right house,' said she, glancing at the lad, and smiling. 'But I was not sure till you opened the door.'

The figure and action were those of the phantom; but her voice was so indescribably sweet, her glance so winning, her smile so tender, so unlike that of Rhoda's midnight visitant, that the latter could hardly believe the evidence of her senses. She was truly glad that she had not hidden away in sheer aversion, as she had been inclined to do. In her basket Mrs Lodge brought the pair of boots that she had promised to the boy, and other useful articles.

At these proofs of a kindly feeling towards her and hers, Rhoda's heart reproached her bitterly. This innocent young thing should have her blessing and not her curse. When she left them a light seemed gone from the dwelling. Two days later she came again to know if the boots fitted; and less than a fortnight after that paid Rhoda another call. On this occasion the boy was absent.

'I walk a good deal,' said Mrs Lodge, 'and your house is the nearest outside our own parish. I hope you are well. You don't look quite well.'

Rhoda said she was well enough; and indeed, though the paler of the two, there was more of the strength that endures in her well-defined features and large frame, than in the soft-cheeked young woman before her. The conversation became quite confidential as regarded their powers and weaknesses; and when Mrs Lodge was leaving, Rhoda said, 'I hope you will find this air agree with you, ma'am, and not suffer from the damp of the water-meads.'

The younger one replied that there was not much doubt of it, her general health being usually good. 'Though, now you remind me,' she added, 'I have one little ailment which puzzles me. It is nothing serious, but I cannot make it out.'

She uncovered her left hand and arm; and their outline confronted Rhoda's gaze as the exact original of the limb she had beheld and seized in her dream. Upon the pink round surface of the arm were faint marks of an unhealthy colour, as if produced by a rough grasp. Rhoda's eyes became riveted on the discolorations; she fancied that she discerned in them the shape of her own four fingers.

'How did it happen?' she said mechanically.

'I cannot tell,' replied Mrs Lodge, shaking her head. 'One night when I was sound asleep, dreaming I was away in some strange place, a pain suddenly shot into my arm there, and was so keen as to awaken me. I must have struck it in the daytime, I suppose, though I don't remember doing so.' She added, laughing, 'I tell my dear husband that it looks just as if he had flown into a rage and struck me there. Oh, I daresay it will soon disappear.'

'Ha, ha! Yes . . . On what night did it come?'

Mrs Lodge considered, and said it would be a fortnight ago on the morrow. 'When I awoke I could not remember where I was,' she added, 'till the clock striking two reminded me.'

She had named the night and the hour of Rhoda's spectral encounter, and Brook felt like a guilty thing. The artless disclosure startled her; she did not reason on the freaks of coincidence; and all the scenery of that ghastly night returned with double vividness to her mind.

'Oh, can it be,' she said to herself, when her visitor had departed, 'that I exercise a malignant power over people against my own will?' She knew that she had been slily called a witch since her fall; but never having understood why that particular stigma had been attached to her, it had passed disregarded. Could this be the explanation, and had such things as this ever happened before?

IV
A SUGGESTION

The summer drew on, and Rhoda Brook almost dreaded to meet Mrs Lodge again, notwithstanding that her feeling for the young wife amounted wellnigh to affection. Something in her own individuality seemed to convict Rhoda of crime. Yet a fatality sometimes would direct the steps of the latter to the outskirts of Holmstoke whenever she left her house for any other purpose than her daily work; and hence it happened that their next encounter was out of doors. Rhoda could not avoid the subject which had so mystified her, and after the first few words she stammered, 'I hope your – arm is well again, ma'am?' She had perceived with consternation that Gertrude Lodge carried her left arm stiffly.

'No; it is not quite well. Indeed it is no better at all; it is rather worse. It pains me dreadfully sometimes.'

'Perhaps you had better go to a doctor, ma'am.'

She replied that she had already seen a doctor. Her husband had insisted upon her going to one. But the surgeon had not seemed to understand the afflicted limb at all; he had told her to bathe it in hot water, and she had bathed it, but the treatment had done no good.

'Will you let me see it?' said the milkwoman.

Mrs Lodge pushed up her sleeve and disclosed the place, which was a few inches above the wrist. As soon as Rhoda Brook saw it, she could hardly preserve her composure. There was nothing of the nature of a wound, but the arm at that point had a shrivelled look, and the outline of the four fingers appeared more distinct than at the former time. Moreover, she fancied that they were imprinted in precisely the relative position of her clutch upon the arm in the trance; the first finger towards Gertrude's wrist, and the fourth towards her elbow.

What the impress resembled seemed to have struck Gertrude herself since their last meeting. 'It looks almost like finger-marks,' she said; adding with a faint laugh, 'my husband says it is as if some witch, or the devil himself, had taken hold of me there, and blasted the flesh.'

Rhoda shivered. 'That's fancy,' she said hurriedly. 'I wouldn't mind it, if I were you.'

'I shouldn't so much mind it,' said the younger, with hesitation, 'if – if I hadn't a notion that it makes my husband – dislike me – no, love me less. Men think so much of personal appearance.'

'Some do – he for one.'

'Yes; and he was very proud of mine, at first.'

'Keep your arm covered from his sight.'

'Ah – he knows the disfigurement is there!' She tried to hide the tears that filled her eyes.

'Well, ma'am, I earnestly hope it will go away soon.'

And so the milkwoman's mind was chained anew to the subject by a horrid sort of spell as she returned home. The sense of having been guilty of an act of malignity increased, affect as she might to ridicule her superstition. In her secret heart Rhoda did not altogether object to a slight diminution of her successor's beauty, by whatever means it had come about; but she did not wish to inflict upon her physical pain. For though this pretty young woman had rendered impossible any reparation which Lodge might have made Rhoda for his past conduct, everything like resentment at the unconscious usurpation had quite passed away from the elder's mind.

If the sweet and kindly Gertrude Lodge only knew of the scene in the bed-chamber, what would she think? Not to inform her of it seemed treachery in the presence of her friendliness; but tell she could not of her own accord – neither could she devise a remedy.

She mused upon the matter the greater part of the night; and the next day, after the morning milking, set out to obtain another glimpse of Gertrude Lodge if she could, being held to her by a gruesome fascination. By watching the house from a distance the milkmaid was presently able to discern the farmer's wife in a ride she was taking alone – probably to join her husband in some distant field. Mrs Lodge perceived her, and cantered in her direction.

'Good morning, Rhoda!' Gertrude said, when she had come up. 'I was going to call.'

Rhoda noticed that Mrs Lodge held the reins with some difficulty.

'I hope – the bad arm,' said Rhoda.

'They tell me there is possibly one way by which I might be able to find out the cause, and so perhaps the cure, of it,' replied the other anxiously. 'It is by going to some clever man over in Egdon Heath. They did not know if he was still alive – and I cannot remember his name at this moment; but they said that you knew more of his movements than anybody else hereabout, and could tell me if he were still to be consulted. Dear me – what was his name? But you know.'

'Not Conjuror Trendle?' said her thin companion, turning pale.

'Trendle – yes. Is he alive?'

'I believe so,' said Rhoda, with reluctance.

'Why do you call him conjuror?'

'Well – they say – they used to say he was a – he had powers other folks have not.'

'Oh, how could my people be so superstitious as to recommend a man of that sort! I thought they meant some medical man. I shall think no more of him.'

Rhoda looked relieved, and Mrs Lodge rode on. The milkwoman had inwardly seen, from the moment she heard of her having been mentioned as a reference for this man, that there must exist a sarcastic feeling among the work-folk that a sorceress would know the whereabouts of the exorcist. They suspected her, then. A short time ago this would have given no concern to a woman of her common-sense. But she had a haunting reason to be superstitious now; and she had been seized with sudden dread that this Conjuror Trendle might name her as the malignant influence which was blasting the fair person of Gertrude, and so lead her friend to hate her for ever, and to treat her as some fiend in human shape.

But all was not over. Two days after, a shadow intruded into the window-pattern thrown on Rhoda Brook's floor by the afternoon sun. The woman opened the door at once, almost breathlessly.

'Are you alone?' said Gertrude. She seemed to be no less harassed and anxious than Brook herself.

'Yes,' said Rhoda.

'The place on my arm seems worse, and troubles me!' the young farmer's wife went on. 'It is so mysterious! I do hope it will not be a permanent blemish. I have again been thinking of what they said about Conjuror Trendle. I don't really believe in such men, but I should not mind just visiting him, from curiosity – though on no account must my husband know. Is it far to where he lives?'

'Yes – five miles,' said Rhoda backwardly. 'In the heart of Egdon.'

'Well, I should have to walk. Could not you go with me to show me the way – say tomorrow afternoon?'

'Oh, not I – that is,' the milkwoman murmured, with a start of dismay. Again the dread seized her that something to do with her fierce act in the dream might be revealed, and her character in the eyes of the most useful friend she had ever had be ruined irretrievably.

Mrs Lodge urged, and Rhoda finally assented, though with much misgiving. Sad as the journey would be to her, she could not conscientiously stand in the way of a possible remedy for her patron's strange affliction. It was agreed that, to escape suspicion of their mystic intent, they should meet at the edge of the heath, at the corner of a plantation which was visible from the spot where they now stood.

V

CONJUROR TRENDLE

By the next afternoon Rhoda would have done anything to escape this inquiry. But she had promised to go.

Moreover, there was a horrid fascination at times in becoming instrumental in throwing such possible light on her own character as would reveal her to be something greater in the occult world than she had ever herself suspected.

She started just before the time of day mentioned between them, and half an hour's brisk walking brought her to the south-eastern extension of the Egdon tract of country, where the fir plantation was. A slight figure, cloaked and veiled, was already there. Rhoda recognized, almost with a shudder, that Mrs Lodge bore her left arm in a sling.

They hardly spoke to each other, and immediately set out on their climb into the interior of this solemn country, which stood high above the rich alluvial soil they had left half an hour before. It was a long walk; thick clouds made the atmosphere dark, though it was as yet only early afternoon; and the wind howled dismally over the hills of the heath – not improbably the same heath which had witnessed the agony of the Wessex King Ina, presented to after-ages as Lear. Gertrude Lodge talked most, Rhoda replying with monosyllabic preoccupation. She had a strange dislike to walking on the side of her companion where hung the afflicted arm, moving round to the other when inadvertently near it. Much heather had been brushed by their feet when they descended upon a cart-track, beside which stood the house of the man they sought.

He did not profess his remedial practices openly, or

care anything about their continuance, his direct interests being those of a dealer in furze, turf, 'sharp sand', and other local products. Indeed, he affected not to believe largely in his own powers, and when warts that had been shown him for cure miraculously disappeared – which it must be owned they infallibly did – he would say lightly, 'Oh, I only drink a glass of grog upon 'em – perhaps it's all chance,' and immediately turn the subject.

He was at home when they arrived, having in fact seen them descending into his valley. He was a grey-bearded man, with a reddish face, and he looked singularly at Rhoda the first moment he beheld her. Mrs Lodge told him her errand; and then with words of self-disparagement he examined her arm.

'Medicine can't cure it,' he said promptly. ''Tis the work of an enemy.'

Rhoda shrank into herself, and drew back.

'An enemy? What enemy?' asked Mrs Lodge.

He shook his head. 'That's best known to yourself,' he said. 'If you like I can show the person to you, though I shall not myself know who it is. I can do no more; and don't wish to do that.'

She pressed him; on which he told Rhoda to wait outside where she stood, and took Mrs Lodge into the room. It opened immediately from the door; and, as the latter remained ajar, Rhoda Brook could see the proceedings without taking part in them. He brought a tumbler from the dresser, nearly filled it with water, and fetching an egg, prepared it in some private way; after which he broke it on the edge of the glass, so that the white went in and the yolk remained. As it was getting gloomy, he took the glass and its contents to the window, and told Gertrude to watch them closely. They leant over the table together, and the milkwoman could see the opaline hue of the egg-fluid changing form as it sank in the water, but she was not near enough to define the shape that it assumed.

'Do you catch the likeness of any face or figure as you look?' demanded the conjuror of the young woman.

She murmured a reply, in tones so low as to be inaudible to Rhoda, and continued to gaze intently into the glass. Rhoda turned, and walked a few steps away.

When Mrs Lodge came out, and her face was met by the light, it appeared exceedingly pale – as pale as Rhoda's – against the sad dun shades of the upland's garniture. Trendle shut the door behind her, and they at once started homeward together. But Rhoda perceived that her companion had quite changed.

'Did he charge much?' she asked tentatively.

'Oh no – nothing. He would not take a farthing,' said Gertrude.

'And what did you see?' inquired Rhoda.

'Nothing I – care to speak of.' The constraint in her manner was remarkable; her face was so rigid as to wear an oldened aspect, faintly suggestive of the face in Rhoda's bed-chamber.

'Was it you who first proposed coming here?' Mrs

Lodge suddenly inquired, after a long pause. 'How very odd, if you did!'

'No. But I am not sorry we have come, all things considered,' she replied. For the first time a sense of triumph possessed her, and she did not altogether deplore that the young thing at her side should learn that their lives had been antagonized by other influences than their own.

The subject was no more alluded to during the long and dreary walk home. But in some way or other a story was whispered about the many-dairied Swenn valley that winter that Mrs Lodge's gradual loss of the use of her left arm was owing to her being 'overlooked' by Rhoda Brook. The latter kept her own counsel about the incubus, but her face grew sadder and thinner; and in the spring she and her boy disappeared from the neighbourhood of Holmstoke.

VI

A SECOND ATTEMPT

Half a dozen years passed away, and Mr and Mrs Lodge's married experience sank into prosiness, and worse. The farmer was usually gloomy and silent: the woman whom he had wooed for her grace and beauty was contorted and disfigured in the left limb; moreover, she had brought him no child, which rendered it likely that he would be the last of a family who had occupied that valley for some two hundred years. He thought of Rhoda Brook and her son; and feared this might be a judgement from heaven upon him.

The once blithe-hearted and enlightened Gertrude was changing into an irritable, superstitious woman, whose whole time was given to experimenting upon her ailment with every quack remedy she came across. She was honestly attached to her husband, and was ever secretly hoping against hope to win back his heart again by regaining some at least of her personal beauty. Hence it arose that her closet was lined with bottles, packets, and ointment-pots of every description – nay, bunches of mystic herbs, charms, and books of necromancy, which in her schoolgirl time she would have ridiculed as folly.

'Damned if you won't poison yourself with these apothecary messes and witch mixtures some time or other,' said her husband, when his eye chanced to fall upon the multitudinous array.

She did not reply, but turned her sad, soft glance upon him in such heart-swollen reproach that he looked sorry for his words, and added, 'I only meant it for your good, you know, Gertrude.'

'I'll clear out the whole lot, and destroy them,' said she huskily, 'and attempt such remedies no more!'

'You want somebody to cheer you,' he observed. 'I once thought of adopting a boy; but he is too old now. And he is gone away I don't know where.'

She guessed to whom he alluded; for Rhoda Brook's

story had in the course of years become known to her; though not a word had ever passed between her husband and herself on the subject. Neither had she ever spoken to him of her visit to Conjuror Trendle, and of what was revealed to her, or she thought was revealed to her, by that solitary heath-man.

She was now five-and-twenty; but she seemed older. 'Six years of marriage, and only a few months of love,' she sometimes whispered to herself. And then she thought of the apparent cause, and said, with a tragic glance at her withering limb, 'If I could only again be as I was when he first saw me!'

She obediently destroyed her nostrums and charms; but there remained a hankering wish to try something else – some other sort of cure altogether. She had never revisited Trendle since she had been conducted to the house of the solitary by Rhoda against her will; but it now suddenly occurred to Gertrude that she would, in a last desperate effort at deliverance from this seeming curse, again seek out the man, if he yet lived. He was entitled to a certain credence, for the indistinct form he had raised in the glass had undoubtedly resembled the only woman in the world who – as she now knew, though not then – could have a reason for bearing her ill-will. The visit should be paid.

This time she went alone, though she nearly got lost on the heath, and roamed a considerable distance out of her way. Trendle's house was reached at last, however:

he was not indoors, and instead of waiting at the cottage she went to where his bent figure was pointed out to her at work a long way off. Trendle remembered her, and laying down the handful of furze-roots which he was gathering and throwing into a heap, he offered to accompany her in her homeward direction, as the distance was considerable and the days were short. So they walked together, his head bowed nearly to the earth, and his form of a colour with it.

'You can send away warts and other excrescences, I know,' she said; 'why can't you send away this?' And the arm was uncovered.

'You think too much of my powers!' said Trendle; 'and I am old and weak now, too. No, no; it is too much for me to attempt in my own person. What have ye tried?'

She named to him some of the hundred medicaments and counterspells which she had adopted from time to time. He shook his head.

'Some were good enough,' he said approvingly; 'but not many of them for such as this. This is of the nature of a blight, not of the nature of a wound; and if you ever do throw it off, it will be all at once.'

'If I only could!'

'There is only one chance of doing it known to me. It has never failed in kindred afflictions, – that I can declare. But it is hard to carry out, and especially for a woman.'

'Tell me!' said she.

'You must touch with the limb the neck of a man who's been hanged.'

She started a little at the image he had raised.

'Before he's cold – just after he's cut down,' continued the conjuror impassively.

'How can that do good?'

'It will turn the blood and change the constitution. But, as I say, to do it is hard. You must get into jail, and wait for him when he's brought off the gallows. Lots have done it, though perhaps not such pretty women as you. I used to send dozens for skin complaints. But that was in former times. The last I sent was in '13 – near twenty years ago.'

He had no more to tell her; and, when he had put her into a straight track homeward, turned and left her, refusing all money as at first.

VII
A RIDE

The communication sank deep into Gertrude's mind. Her nature was rather a timid one; and probably of all remedies that the white wizard could have suggested there was not one which would have filled her with so much aversion as this, not to speak of the immense obstacles in the way of its adoption.

Casterbridge, the county-town, was a dozen or fifteen

miles off; and though in those days, when men were executed for horse-stealing, arson, and burglary, an assize seldom passed without a hanging, it was not likely that she could get access to the body of the criminal unaided. And the fear of her husband's anger made her reluctant to breathe a word of Trendle's suggestion to him or to anybody about him.

She did nothing for months, and patiently bore her disfigurement as before. But her woman's nature, craving for renewed love, through the medium of renewed beauty (she was but twenty-five), was ever stimulating her to try what, at any rate, could hardly do her any harm. 'What came by a spell will go by a spell surely,' she would say. Whenever her imagination pictured the act she shrank in terror from the possibility of it: then the words of the conjuror, 'It will turn your blood,' were seen to be capable of a scientific no less than a ghastly interpretation; the mastering desire returned, and urged her on again.

There was at this time but one county paper, and that her husband only occasionally borrowed. But old-fashioned days had old-fashioned means, and news was extensively conveyed by word of mouth from market to market or from fair to fair; so that, whenever such an event as an execution was about to take place, few within a radius of twenty miles were ignorant of the coming sight; and, so far as Holmstoke was concerned, some enthusiasts had been known to walk all the way to Casterbridge and back in one day, solely to witness the spectacle. The next assizes were in March; and when Gertrude Lodge heard that they had been held, she inquired stealthily at the inn as to the result, as soon as she could find opportunity.

She was, however, too late. The time at which the sentences were to be carried out had arrived, and to make the journey and obtain admission at such short notice required at least her husband's assistance. She dared not tell him, for she had found by delicate experiment that these smouldering village beliefs made him furious if mentioned, partly because he half entertained them himself. It was therefore necessary to wait for another opportunity.

Her determination received a fillip from learning that two epileptic children had attended from this very village of Holmstoke many years before with beneficial results, though the experiment had been strongly condemned by the neighbouring clergy. April, May, June passed; and it is no overstatement to say that by the end of the last-named month Gertrude wellnigh longed for the death of a fellow-creature. Instead of her formal prayers each night, her unconscious prayer was, 'O Lord, hang some guilty or innocent person soon!'

This time she made earlier inquiries, and was altogether more systematic in her proceedings. Moreover, the season was summer, between the haymaking and the harvest, and in the leisure thus afforded her husband had been holiday-taking away from home.

The assizes were in July, and she went to the inn as before. There was to be one execution – only one – for arson.

Her greatest problem was not how to get to Casterbridge, but what means she should adopt for obtaining admission to the jail. Though access for such purposes had formerly never been denied, the custom had fallen into desuetude; and in contemplating her possible difficulties, she was again almost driven to fall back upon her husband. But, on sounding him about the assizes, he was so uncommunicative, so more than usually cold, that she did not proceed, and decided that whatever she did she would do alone.

Fortune, obdurate hitherto, showed her unexpected favour. On the Thursday before the Saturday fixed for the execution, Lodge remarked to her that he was going away from home for another day or two on business at a fair, and that he was sorry he could not take her with him.

She exhibited on this occasion so much readiness to stay at home that he looked at her in surprise. Time had been when she would have shown deep disappointment at the loss of such a jaunt. However, he lapsed into his usual taciturnity, and on the day named left Holmstoke.

It was now her turn. She at first had thought of driving, but on reflection held that driving would not do, since it would necessitate her keeping to the turnpike-road, and so increase by tenfold the risk of her ghastly errand being found out. She decided to ride, and avoid the beaten track, notwithstanding that in her husband's stables there was no animal just at present which by any stretch of imagination could be considered a lady's mount, in spite of his promise before marriage to always keep a mare for her. He had, however, many horses, fine ones of their kind; and among the rest was a serviceable creature, an equine Amazon, with a back as broad as a sofa, on which Gertrude had occasionally taken an airing when unwell. This horse she chose.

On Friday afternoon one of the men brought it round. She was dressed, and before going down looked at her shrivelled arm. 'Ah!' she said to it, 'if it had not been for you this terrible ordeal would have been saved me!'

When strapping up the bundle in which she carried a few articles of clothing, she took occasion to say to the servant, 'I take these in case I should not get back tonight from the person I am going to visit. Don't be alarmed if I am not in by ten, and close up the house as usual. I shall be at home tomorrow for certain.' She meant then to privately tell her husband: the deed accomplished was not like the deed projected. He would almost certainly forgive her.

And then the pretty palpitating Gertrude Lodge went from her husband's homestead; but though her goal was Casterbridge she did not take the direct route thither through Stickleford. Her cunning course at first was in precisely the opposite direction. As soon as she was out of sight, however, she turned to the left, by a road which led into Egdon, and on entering the heath wheeled round, and set out in the true course, due westerly. A more private way down the county could not be imagined; and as to direction, she had merely to keep her horse's head to a point a little to the right of the sun. She knew that she would light upon a furze-cutter or cottager of some sort from time to time, from whom she might correct her bearing.

Though the date was comparatively recent, Egdon was much less fragmentary in character than now. The attempts – successful and otherwise – at cultivation on the lower slopes, which intrude and break up the original heath into small detached heaths, had not been carried far: Enclosure Acts had not taken effect, and the banks and fences which now exclude the cattle of those villagers who formerly enjoyed rights of commonage thereon, and the carts of those who had turbary privileges which kept them in firing all the year round, were not erected. Gertrude therefore rode along with no other obstacles than the prickly furze-bushes, the mats of heather, the white water-courses, and the natural steeps and declivities of the ground.

Her horse was sure, if heavy-footed and slow, and though a draught animal, was easy-paced; had it been otherwise, she was not a woman who could have ventured to ride over such a bit of country with a half-dead arm. It was therefore nearly eight o'clock when she drew rein to breathe the mare on the last outlying high point of heath-land towards Casterbridge, previous to leaving Egdon for the cultivated valleys.

She halted before a pond, flanked by the ends of two hedges; a railing ran through the centre of the pond, dividing it in half. Over the railing she saw the low green country; over the green trees the roofs of the town; over the roofs a white flat facade, denoting the entrance to the county jail. On the roof of this front specks were moving about; they seemed to be workmen erecting something. Her flesh crept. She descended slowly, and was soon amid corn-fields and pastures. In another half-hour, when it was almost dusk, Gertrude reached the White Hart, the first inn of the town on that side.

Little surprise was excited by her arrival: farmers' wives rode on horseback then more than they do now; though, for that matter, Mrs Lodge was not imagined to be a wife at all; the inn-keeper supposed her some harum-skarum young woman who had come to attend 'hang-fair' next day. Neither her husband nor herself ever dealt in Casterbridge market, so that she was unknown. While dismounting she beheld a crowd of boys standing at the door of a harness-maker's shop just above the inn, looking inside it with deep interest.

'What is going on there?' she asked of the ostler.

'Making the rope for tomorrow.'

She throbbed responsively, and contracted her arm.

' 'Tis sold by the inch afterwards,' the man continued. 'I could get you a bit, miss, for nothing, if you'd like?'

She hastily repudiated any such wish, all the more from a curious creeping feeling that the condemned wretch's destiny was becoming interwoven with her own; and having engaged a room for the night sat down to think.

Up to this time she had formed but the vaguest notions about her means of obtaining access to the prison. The words of the cunning-man returned to her mind. He had implied that she should use her beauty, impaired though it was, as a pass-key. In her inexperience she knew little about jail functionaries; she had heard of a high-sheriff and an under-sheriff, but dimly only. She knew, however, that there must be a hangman, and to the hangman she determined to apply.

VIII
A WATER-SIDE HERMIT

At this date, and for several years after, there was a hangman to almost every jail. Gertrude found, on inquiry, that the Casterbridge official dwelt in a lonely cottage by a deep slow river flowing under the cliff on which the prison buildings were situate – the stream being the self-same one, though she did not know it, which watered the Stickleford and Holmstoke meads lower down in its course.

Having changed her dress, and before she had eaten or drunk – for she could not take her ease till she had ascertained some particulars – Gertrude pursued her way by a path along the water-side to the cottage indicated. Passing thus the outskirts of the jail, she discerned on the level roof over the gateway three rectangular lines against the sky, where the specks had been moving in her distant view; she recognized what the erection was, and passed quickly on. Another hundred yards brought her to the executioner's house, which a boy pointed out. It stood close to the same stream, and was hard by a weir, the waters of which emitted a steady roar.

While she stood hesitating the door opened, and an old man came forth shading a candle with one hand. Locking the door on the outside, he turned to a flight of wooden steps fixed against the end of the cottage, and began to ascend them, this being evidently the staircase to his bedroom. Gertrude hastened forward, but by the time she reached the foot of the ladder he was at the top. She called to him loudly enough to be heard above the roar of the weir; he looked down and said, 'What d'ye want here?'

'To speak to you a minute.'

The candle-light, such as it was, fell upon her imploring, pale, upturned face, and Davies (as the hangman was called) backed down the ladder. 'I was just going to bed,' he said; '"Early to bed and early to rise," but I don't mind stopping a minute for such a one as you. Come into the house.' He reopened the door, and preceded her to the room within.

The implements of his daily work, which was that of a

jobbing gardener, stood in a corner, and seeing probably that she looked rural, he said, 'If you want me to undertake country work I can't come, for I never leave Casterbridge for gentle nor simple – not I. Though sometimes I make others leave,' he added formally.

'Yes, yes! That's it! Tomorrow!'

'Ah! I thought so. Well, what's the matter about that? 'Tis no use to come here about the knot – folks do come continually, but I tell 'em one knot is as merciful as another if ye keep it under the ear. Is the unfortunate man a relation; or, I should say, perhaps' (looking at her dress) 'a person who's been in your employ?'

'No. What time is the execution?'

'The same as usual – twelve o'clock, or as soon after as the London mail-coach gets in. We always wait for that, in case of a reprieve.'

'Oh – a reprieve – I hope not!' she said involuntarily.

'Well, – he, he! – as a matter of business, so do I! But still, if ever a young fellow deserved to be let off, this one does; only just turned eighteen, and only present by chance when the rick was fired. Howsomever, there's not much risk of it, as they are obliged to make an example of him, there having been so much destruction of property that way lately.'

'I mean,' she explained, 'that I want to touch him for a charm, a cure of an affliction, by the advice of a man who has proved the virtue of the remedy.'

'Oh yes, miss! Now I understand. I've had such people

come in past years. But it didn't strike me that you looked of a sort to require blood-turning. What's the complaint? The wrong kind for this, I'll be bound.'

'My arm.' She reluctantly showed the withered skin.

'Ah! – 'tis all a-scram!' said the hangman, examining it.

'Yes,' said she.

'Well,' he continued with interest, 'that *is* the class o' subject, I'm bound to admit! I like the look of the place; it is truly as suitable for the cure as any I ever saw. 'Twas a knowing-man that sent 'ee, whoever he was.'

'You can contrive for me all that's necessary?' she said breathlessly.

'You should really have gone to the governor of the jail, and your doctor with 'ee, and given your name and address – that's how it used to be done, if I recollect. Still, perhaps, I can manage it for a trifling fee.'

'Oh, thank you! I would rather do it this way, as I should like it kept private.'

'Lover not to know, eh?'

'No – husband.'

'Aha! Very well. I'll get 'ee a touch of the corpse.'

'Where is it now?' she said, shuddering.

'It? – *he*, you mean; he's living yet. Just inside that little small winder up there in the glum.' He signified the jail on the cliff above.

She thought of her husband and her friends. 'Yes, of course,' she said; 'and how am I to proceed?'

He took her to the door. 'Now, do you be waiting at

the little wicket in the wall, that you'll find up there in the lane, not later than one o'clock. I will open it from the inside, as I shan't come home to dinner till he's cut down. Good night. Be punctual; and if you don't want anybody to know 'ee, wear a veil. Ah – once I had such a daughter as you!'

She went away, and climbed the path above, to assure herself that she would be able to find the wicket next day. Its outline was soon visible to her – a narrow opening in the outer wall of the prison precincts. The steep was so great that, having reached the wicket, she stopped a moment to breathe; and, looking back upon the water-side cot, saw the hangman again ascending his outdoor staircase. He entered the loft or chamber to which it led, and in a few minutes extinguished his light.

The town clock struck ten, and she returned to the White Hart as she had come.

IX
A RENCOUNTER

It was one o'clock on Saturday. Gertrude Lodge, having been admitted to the jail as above described, was sitting in a waiting-room within the second gate, which stood under a classic archway of ashlar, then comparatively modern, and bearing the inscription, 'COVNTY JAIL: 1793.' This had been the facade she saw from the heath the day before. Near at hand was a passage to the roof on which the gallows stood.

The town was thronged, and the market suspended; but Gertrude had seen scarcely a soul. Having kept her room till the hour of the appointment, she had proceeded to the spot by a way which avoided the open space below the cliff where the spectators had gathered; but she could, even now, hear the multitudinous babble of their voices, out of which rose at intervals the hoarse croak of a single voice, uttering the words, 'Last dying speech and confession!' There had been no reprieve, and the execution was over; but the crowd still waited to see the body taken down.

Soon the persistent girl heard a trampling overhead, then a hand beckoned to her, and, following directions, she went out and crossed the inner paved court beyond the gatehouse, her knees trembling so that she could scarcely walk. One of her arms was out of its sleeve, and only covered by her shawl.

On the spot at which she had now arrived were two trestles, and before she could think of their purpose she heard heavy feet descending stairs somewhere at her back. Turn her head she would not, or could not, and, rigid in this position, she was conscious of a rough coffin passing her shoulder, borne by four men. It was open, and in it lay the body of a young man, wearing the smockfrock of a rustic, and fustian breeches. It had been thrown into the coffin so hastily that the skirt of the smockfrock was hanging over. The burden was temporarily deposited on the trestles.

By this time the young woman's state was such that a grey mist seemed to float before her eyes, on account of which, and the veil she wore, she could scarcely discern anything: it was as though she had nearly died, but was held up by a sort of galvanism.

'Now,' said a voice close at hand, and she was just conscious that it had been addressed to her.

By a last strenuous effort she advanced, at the same time hearing persons approaching behind her. She bared her poor curst arm; and Davies, uncovering the face of the corpse, took Gertrude's hand, and held it so that her arm lay across the dead man's neck, upon a line the colour of an unripe blackberry, which surrounded it.

Gertrude shrieked: 'the turn o' the blood,' predicted by the conjuror, had taken place. But at that moment a second shriek rent the air of the enclosure: it was not Gertrude's, and its effect upon her was to make her start round.

Immediately behind her stood Rhoda Brook, her face drawn, and her eyes red with weeping. Behind Rhoda stood her own husband; his countenance lined, his eyes dim, but without a tear.

'D—n you! what are you doing here?' he said hoarsely.

'Hussy – to come between us and our child now!' cried Rhoda. 'This is the meaning of what Satan showed me in the vision! You are like her at last!' And clutching the bare arm of the younger woman, she pulled her unresistingly back against the wall. Immediately Brook had loosened her hold the fragile young Gertrude slid down against the feet of her husband. When he lifted her up she was unconscious.

The mere sight of the twain had been enough to suggest to her that the dead young man was Rhoda's son. At that time the relatives of an executed convict had the privilege of claiming the body for burial, if they chose to do so; and it was for this purpose that Lodge was awaiting the inquest with Rhoda. He had been summoned by her as soon as the young man was taken in the crime, and at different times since; and he had attended in court during the trial. This was the 'holiday' he had been indulging in of late. The two wretched parents had wished to avoid exposure; and hence had come themselves for the body, a waggon and sheet for its conveyance and covering being in waiting outside.

Gertrude's case was so serious that it was deemed advisable to call to her the surgeon who was at hand. She was taken out of the jail into the town; but she never reached home alive. Her delicate vitality, sapped perhaps by the paralysed arm, collapsed under the double shock that followed the severe strain, physical and mental, to which she had subjected herself during the previous twenty-four hours. Her blood had been 'turned' indeed – too far. Her death took place in the town three days after.

Her husband was never seen in Casterbridge again;

once only in the old marketplace at Anglebury, which he had so much frequented, and very seldom in public anywhere. Burdened at first with moodiness and remorse, he eventually changed for the better, and appeared as a chastened and thoughtful man. Soon after attending the funeral of his poor young wife he took steps towards giving up the farms in Holmstoke and the adjoining parish, and, having sold every head of his stock, he went away to Port-Bredy, at the other end of the county, living there in solitary lodgings till his death two years later of a painless decline. It was then found that he had bequeathed the whole of his not inconsiderable property to a reformatory for boys, subject to the payment of a small annuity to Rhoda Brook, if she could be found to claim it.

For some time she could not be found; but eventually she reappeared in her old parish, – absolutely refusing, however, to have anything to do with the provision made for her. Her monotonous milking at the dairy was resumed, and followed for many long years, till her form became bent, and her once abundant dark hair white and worn away at the forehead – perhaps by long pressure against the cows. Here, sometimes, those who knew her experiences would stand and observe her, and wonder what sombre thoughts were beating inside that impassive, wrinkled brow, to the rhythm of the alternating milk-streams.

The Thieves Who Couldn't Help Sneezing

Many years ago, when oak-trees now past their prime were about as large as elderly gentlemen's walking-sticks, there lived in Wessex a yeoman's son, whose name was Hubert. He was about fourteen years of age, and was as remarkable for his candour and lightness of heart as for his physical courage, of which, indeed, he was a little vain.

One cold Christmas Eve his father, having no other help at hand, sent him on an important errand to a small town several miles from home. He travelled on horseback, and was detained by the business till a late hour of the evening. At last, however, it was completed; he returned to the inn, the horse was saddled, and he started on his way. His journey homeward lay through the Vale of Blackmore, a fertile but somewhat lonely district, with heavy clay roads and crooked lanes. In those days, too, a great part of it was thickly wooded.

It must have been about nine o'clock when, riding along amid the overhanging trees upon his stout-legged cob Jerry, and singing a Christmas carol, to be in harmony with the season, Hubert fancied that he heard a noise among the boughs. This recalled to his mind that the spot he was traversing bore an evil name. Men had been waylaid there. He looked at Jerry, and wished he had been of any other colour than light grey; for on this account the docile animal's form was visible even here in the dense shade. 'What do I care?' he said aloud, after a few minutes of reflection. 'Jerry's legs are too nimble to allow any highwayman to come near me.'

'Ha! ha! indeed,' was said in a deep voice; and the next moment a man darted from the thicket on his right hand, another man from the thicket on his left hand, and another from a tree-trunk a few yards ahead. Hubert's bridle was seized, he was pulled from his horse, and although he struck out with all his might, as a brave boy would naturally do, he was overpowered. His arms were tied behind him, his legs bound tightly together, and he was thrown into the ditch. The robbers, whose faces he could now dimly perceive to be artificially blackened, at once departed, leading off the horse.

As soon as Hubert had a little recovered himself, he found that by great exertion he was able to extricate his legs from the cord; but, in spite of every endeavour, his arms remained bound as fast as before. All, therefore, that he could do was to rise to his feet and proceed on his way with his arms behind him, and trust to chance for getting them unfastened. He knew that it would be impossible to reach home on foot that night, and in such a condition; but he walked on. Owing to the confusion which this attack caused in his brain, he lost his way, and would have been inclined to lie down and rest till morning among the dead leaves had he not known the danger of sleeping without wrappers in a frost so severe. So he wandered further onwards, his arms wrung and numbed by the cord which pinioned him and his heart aching for the loss of poor Jerry, who never had been known to kick, or bite, or show a single vicious habit. He was not a little glad when he discerned through the trees a distant light. Towards this he made his way, and presently found himself in front of a large mansion with flanking wings, gables, and towers, the battlements and chimneys showing their shapes against the stars.

All was silent; but the door stood wide open, it being from this door that the light shone which had attracted him. On entering he found himself in a vast apartment arranged as a dining-hall, and brilliantly illuminated. The walls were covered with a great deal of dark wainscoting, formed into moulded panels, carvings, closet-doors, and the usual fittings of a house of that kind. But what drew his attention most was the large table in the midst of the hall, upon which was spread a sumptuous supper, as yet untouched. Chairs were placed around, and it appeared as if something had occurred to interrupt the meal just at the time when all were ready to begin.

Even had Hubert been so inclined, he could not have eaten in his helpless state, unless by dipping his mouth in the dishes, like a pig or cow. He wished first to obtain assistance; and was about to penetrate further into the house for that purpose when he heard hasty footsteps in the porch and the words, 'Be quick!' uttered in the deep voice which had reached him when he was dragged from the horse. There was only just time for him to dart under the table before three men entered the dining-hall. Peeping from beneath the hanging edges of the tablecloth, he perceived that their faces, too, were blackened, which at once removed any remaining doubts he may have felt that these were the same thieves.

'Now, then,' said the first – the man with the deep voice – 'let us hide ourselves. They will all be back again in a minute. That was a good trick to get them out of the house – eh?'

'Yes. You well imitated the cries of a man in distress,' said the second.

'Excellently,' said the third.

'But they will soon find out that it was a false alarm. Come, where shall we hide? It must be some place we can stay in for two or three hours, till all are in bed and asleep. Ah! I have it. Come this way! I have learnt that the further closet is not opened once in a twelvemonth; it will serve our purpose exactly.'

The speaker advanced into a corridor which led from the hall. Creeping a little farther forward, Hubert could discern that the closet stood at the end, facing the dining-hall. The thieves entered it, and closed the door. Hardly breathing, Hubert glided forward, to learn a little more of their intention, if possible; and, coming close, he could hear the robbers whispering about the different rooms where the jewels, plate, and other valuables of the house were kept, which they plainly meant to steal.

They had not been long in hiding when a gay chattering of ladies and gentlemen was audible on the terrace without. Hubert felt that it would not do to be caught prowling about the house, unless he wished to be taken for a robber himself; and he slipped softly back to the hall, out at the door, and stood in a dark corner of the porch, where he could see everything without being himself seen. In a moment or two a whole troop of personages came gliding past him into the house. There were an elderly gentleman and lady, eight or nine young ladies, as many young men, besides half-a-dozen men-servants and maids. The mansion had apparently been quite emptied of its occupants.

'Now, children and young people, we will resume our meal,' said the old gentleman. 'What the noise could have been I cannot understand. I never felt so certain in my life that there was a person being murdered outside my door.'

Then the ladies began saying how frightened they had been, and how they had expected an adventure, and how it had ended in nothing after all.

'Wait a while,' said Hubert to himself. 'You'll have adventure enough by-and-by, ladies.'

It appeared that the young men and women were married sons and daughters of the old couple, who had come that day to spend Christmas with their parents.

The door was then closed, Hubert being left outside in the porch. He thought this a proper moment for asking their assistance; and, since he was unable to knock with his hands, began boldly to kick the door.

'Hullo! What disturbance are you making here?' said a footman who opened it; and seizing Hubert by the shoulder, he pulled him into the dining-hall. 'Here's a strange boy I have found making a noise in the porch, Sir Simon.'

Everybody turned.

'Bring him forward,' said Sir Simon, the old gentleman before mentioned. 'What were you doing there, my boy?'

'Why, his arms are tied!' said one of the ladies.

'Poor fellow!' said another.

Hubert at once began to explain that he had been waylaid on his journey home, robbed of his horse, and mercilessly left in this condition by the thieves.

'Only to think of it!' exclaimed Sir Simon.

'That's a likely story,' said one of the gentleman-guests, incredulously.

'Doubtful, hey?' asked Sir Simon.

'Perhaps he's a robber himself,' suggested a lady.

'There is a curiously wild wicked look about him, certainly, now that I examine him closely,' said the old mother.

Hubert blushed with shame; and, instead of continuing his story, and relating that the robbers were concealed in the house, he doggedly held his tongue, and half resolved to let them find out their danger for themselves.

'Well, untie him,' said Sir Simon. 'Come, since it is Christmas Eve, we'll treat him well. Here, my lad; sit down in that empty seat at the bottom of the table, and make as good a meal as you can. When you have had your fill we will listen to more particulars of your story.'

The feast then proceeded; and Hubert, now at liberty, was not at all sorry to join in. The more they ate and drank the merrier did the company become; the wine flowed freely, the logs flared up the chimney, the ladies laughed at the gentlemen's stories; in short, all went as noisily and as happily as a Christmas gathering in old times possibly could do.

Hubert, in spite of his hurt feelings at their doubts of his honesty, could not help being warmed both in mind and in body by the good cheer, the scene, and the example of hilarity set by his neighbours. At last he laughed as heartily at their stories and repartees as the old Baronet, Sir Simon, himself. When the meal was almost over one of the sons, who had drunk a little too much wine, after the manner of men in that century, said to Hubert, 'Well, my boy, how are you? Can you take a pinch of snuff?' He held out one of the snuff-boxes which were then becoming common among young and old throughout the country.

'Thank you,' said Hubert, accepting a pinch.

'Tell the ladies who you are, what you are made of, and

what you can do,' the young man continued, slapping Hubert upon the shoulder.

'Certainly,' said our hero, drawing himself up, and thinking it best to put a bold face on the matter. 'I am a travelling magician.'

'Indeed!'

'What shall we hear next?'

'Can you call up spirits from the vasty deep, young wizard?'

'I can conjure up a tempest in a cupboard,' Hubert replied.

'Ha-ha!' said the old Baronet, pleasantly rubbing his hands. 'We must see this performance. Girls, don't go away: here's something to be seen.'

'Not dangerous, I hope?' said the old lady.

Hubert rose from the table. 'Hand me your snuff-box, please,' he said to the young man who had made free with him. 'And now,' he continued, 'without the least noise, follow me. If any of you speak it will break the spell.'

They promised obedience. He entered the corridor, and, taking off his shoes, went on tiptoe to the closet door, the guests advancing in a silent group at a little distance behind him. Hubert next placed a stool in front of the door, and, by standing upon it, was tall enough to reach to the top. He then, just as noiselessly, poured all the snuff from the box along the upper edge of the door, and, with a few short puffs of breath, blew the snuff through the chink into the interior of the closet. He held up his finger to the assembly, that they might be silent.

'Dear me, what's that?' said the old lady, after a minute or two had elapsed.

A suppressed sneeze had come from inside the closet.

Hubert held up his finger again.

'How very singular,' whispered Sir Simon. 'This is most interesting.'

Hubert took advantage of the moment to gently slide the bolt of the closet door into its place. 'More snuff,' he said, calmly.

'More snuff,' said Sir Simon. Two or three gentlemen passed their boxes, and the contents were blown in at that top of the closet. Another sneeze, not quite so well suppressed as the first, was heard: then another, which seemed to say that it would not be suppressed under any circumstances whatever. At length there arose a perfect storm of sneezes.

'Excellent, excellent for one so young!' said Sir Simon. 'I am much interested in this trick of throwing the voice – called, I believe, ventriloquism.'

'More snuff,' said Hubert.

'More snuff,' said Sir Simon. Sir Simon's man brought a large jar of the best scented Scotch.

Hubert once more charged the upper chink of the closet, and blew the snuff into the interior, as before. Again he charged, and again, emptying the whole contents of the jar. The tumults of sneezes became really extraordinary to listen to – there was no cessation. It was like wind, rain, and sea, battling in a hurricane.

'I believe there are men inside, and that it is no trick at all!' exclaimed Sir Simon, the truth flashing on him.

'There are,' said Hubert. 'They are come to rob the house; and they are the same who stole my horse.'

The sneezes changed to spasmodic groans. One of the thieves, hearing Hubert's voice, cried, 'Oh! mercy! mercy! let us out of this!'

'Where's my horse?' said Hubert.

'Tied to the tree in the hollow behind Short's Gibbet. Mercy! mercy! let us out, or we shall die of suffocation!'

All the Christmas guests now perceived that this was no longer sport, but serious earnest. Guns and cudgels were procured; all the men-servants were called in, and arranged in position outside the closet. At a signal Hubert withdrew the bolt, and stood on the defensive. But the three robbers, far from attacking them, were found crouching in the corner, gasping for breath. They made no resistance; and, being pinioned, were placed in an out-house till the morning.

Hubert now gave the remainder of his story to the assembled company, and was profusely thanked for the services he had rendered. Sir Simon pressed him to stay over the night, and accept the use of the best bed-room the house afforded, which had been occupied by Queen Elizabeth and King Charles successively when on their visits to this part of the country. But Hubert declined, being anxious to find his horse Jerry, and to test the truth of the robbers' statements concerning him.

Several of the guests accompanied Hubert to the spot behind the gibbet, alluded to by the thieves as where Jerry was hidden. When they reached the knoll and looked over, behold! there the horse stood, uninjured, and quite unconcerned. At sight of Hubert he neighed joyfully; and nothing could exceed Hubert's gladness at finding him. He mounted, wished his friends 'Good night!' and cantered off in the direction they pointed out as his nearest way, reaching home safely about four o'clock in the morning.

PENGUIN

LITTLE BLACK

CLASSICS

“她露出她那只被诅咒的
可怜的胳膊……”

PENGUIN
LITTLE BLACK
CLASSICS

萎缩的胳膊

The Withered Arm

[英] 托马斯·哈代 著

张玲 张扬 谢万容 译

中信出版集团 · 北京

图书在版编目（C I P）数据

企鹅经典·小黑书.第一辑：英、汉 /（日）吉田兼好等著；文东等译. -- 北京：中信出版社，2018.11（2022.7 重印）
书名原文：Penguin Little Black Classics
ISBN 978-7-5086-9400-9

Ⅰ.①企… Ⅱ.①吉… ②文… Ⅲ.①世界文学一作品综合集一英、汉 Ⅳ.①I11

中国版本图书馆 CIP 数据核字 (2018) 第 193780 号

企鹅经典：小黑书　第一辑
萎缩的胳膊

著　　者：［英］托马斯·哈代
译　　者：张玲 张扬 谢万容
出版发行：中信出版集团股份有限公司
（北京市朝阳区惠新东街甲 4 号富盛大厦 2 座 邮编 100029）
承 印 者：河北鹏润印刷有限公司

开　　本：787mm×1092mm　1/32　　印　　张：41　　字　　数：300 千字
版　　次：2018 年 11 月第 1 版　　印　　次：2022 年 7 月第13次印刷
京权图字：01-2018-6477
书　　号：ISBN 978-7-5086-9400-9
定　　价：149.00 元（全 10 册）

服务热线：400-600-8099
投稿邮箱：author@citicpub.com

目录

萎缩的胳膊

一　遭遗弃的挤奶姑娘

这是一个有八十头奶牛的牛奶场，一群挤奶工，正式的和临时的，都在干活儿；季节虽然还不过是四月初的春天，可放牧全在那些水浇地牧场上，所以那些奶牛个个都是“满桶奶的”。时间大约到了傍晚六点钟，那些大个头、红颜色、长方块的畜生，有四分之三已经挤完了奶，这样大家就有机会聊聊天了。

“我听说，他明天真要把新娘子带回家来啦。他们今天已经从安格伯瑞动身了。”

声音仿佛发自那头叫作樱桃的母牛的肚子，不过说

话的人可是一个挤奶妇，她的脸埋在那头一动不动的母牛肋条上。

“有谁瞧见过她吗？”另一个人问。

先说话的那个人说，没有。“可他们说，她真够得上是玫瑰脸蛋儿，樱草花球小身段儿。”她又这样加了一句。这个挤奶妇一边说，一边转过脸去，这样，她就可以隔着她那头母牛的尾巴对场院的那一边瞟上一眼。那里有一个姿容憔悴的瘦削女人，大约三十岁模样，和别人多少分开了一点，正在挤奶。

“他们说，比他小好些岁呢。”第二个人接着说，也对那个方向投去若有所思的一瞥。

“那么，你说他多大岁数了？”

“三十上下吧。”

“更像四十岁。”旁边一个年岁大的挤奶男工插了一句，他罩了一件大白围裙或者说“工作罩衣”，帽檐向下耷拉着，看起来像是一个女人。“他出世的时候，水坝还没筑，我在那里提水的时候，还没拿大人的工资呢。”

议论越来越热闹，牛奶往下流的声音变得断断续续的了，这时从另一头母牛肚子那儿传来颇有权威的声音：“嗨，嗨，农场主洛吉的年纪，或者洛吉的新太太，究

竟和咱们有啥关系？不管他或者她是多大岁数，反正我租他的这些奶牛，每头牛每年都得交他九镑。接着干你们的活儿吧，要不，咱们干不完天就黑了。晚霞已经把天都照红啦。”说这话的人是牛奶场的老板，这些挤奶的女工和男工都是他雇的。

谁也没有再公然大声议论农场主洛吉的婚事了，不过第一个说话的女工仍在她那头牛下面对她的近邻嘀咕：“她可不好受啦。”她指的是刚才提到的那个瘦削憔悴的挤奶女工。

“啊，不会的，”第二个说，“他已经有几年没跟若达·布茹克说话了。”

挤完了奶，他们刷净了自己的奶桶，把它们挂在奶桶架上。它像通常的奶桶架一样，是用一根剥了皮的橡树枝做的，上面装着许多钩子，直直地竖在地上，像一盘巨大的鹿角。大多数人都朝着四面八方回家去了。那个一言未发的瘦女人，和一个大约十二岁的男孩走到一起，他们俩也顺着那块场地走上去了。

他们走的路和别人不同，通向水浇牧场上面一块高出来的孤零零的地方，离爱敦荒原的边缘不远，当他们走到家门附近的时候，可以远远看见荒原那黑乎乎的

影子。

“他们刚才在场院里说，你爸爸明天要把他那个年轻的媳妇从安格伯瑞带回来了，”那个女人说，“我想打发你到市场上去干点事，你准保可以碰见他们。”

“好吧，妈妈，”男孩说，“那么爸爸结婚了吗？”

“是……你可以看她一眼。要是你真看到她了，就告诉我她什么样。”

“好吧，妈妈。”

“她是长得黑还是白，个儿高不高——是不是跟我一样高。还有，她看起来是不是像一个靠干活儿吃饭的女人，或者是一个富裕惯了的人，从来没有干过什么活儿，显出一副太太的样子，就像我想的那样。”

“好。”

他们在苍茫暮色中爬上那座小山，走进自己的农舍。农舍四面是土墙，多次雨水冲刷，已经把墙面冲出一道道的沟纹和凹洼，原来那种平整的墙面，一点也看不见了，而上面铺草的房顶，时而露出一根椽子，像是一根骨头戳破了皮肤露在外面。

她跪在炉灶旁边，两块泥煤架在前面，煤块中间放着石楠的干枝，她用力吹那堆红热的余烬，一直吹到泥

煤燃起了火苗。火光照亮了她苍白的脸颊，使她那对曾经看起来很漂亮的眼睛，好像又漂亮起来了。“是的，”她接着又说起来，“看她长得是黑还是白，还有，要是能够看得到，留神一下她那双手白不白，要是不白，就看看它们是不是做过家务活儿，或者是像我这双挤奶的手。”

男孩照样答应了，这次有点心不在焉，他母亲没有注意到，他正在用一把小刀，在山毛榉木靠背椅上刻一道凹痕。

二　年轻媳妇

从安格伯瑞到霍姆斯托克的大道，基本都是平路，只有一个地方有个很陡的上坡道，使它显得不那么单调。赶集回家的农夫，都是一路让马小跑着，到了这段短短的陡坡，才赶着马缓慢爬坡。

第二天黄昏，太阳还挺亮，一辆崭新漂亮的轻便双轮马车，由一匹健壮的牝马拉着，沿着那条平川大道向西飞跑。这辆车车身是柠檬色的，车轮是红色的。赶车人是个年富力强的自耕农，胡子刮得干干净净，像个演戏的，脸色红里透青。一个兴旺发达的农夫，在镇上

做了几笔顺手的买卖回家，常常就是这样满面生辉。他身旁坐着一个女人，比他年轻得多，简直可以说还是一个女孩儿。她的脸色也很光鲜，但那完全是另外一种性质——柔媚缥缈，像是从一堆玫瑰花瓣透过来的光辉。

没有什么人这样赶路，因为这不是一条主要的大道。在这条沙砾铺成的白色长带上，他们前面空空荡荡，只有一个几乎并不活动的小黑点，它渐渐地变成了一个男孩的模样，好似一只蜗牛正在慢慢向上爬，而且不断地回过头来朝后面张望。他背的那个沉重的包，如果说不是他步履缓慢的理由，也可以说是某种借口。那辆欢腾跳跃的轻便马车，来到前面提到的那个陡坡下面，放慢了速度，这时那个步行的男孩在前面不过几码[1]的地方。他一只手放在屁股上托着那个大包，和马并排走着，同时回过头来，死死盯住农场主的媳妇，好像要把她仔仔细细琢磨个透似的。

夕阳迎面照在她的脸上，把她五官的每一个部分，从她那小巧鼻孔的曲线直到她那双眼睛的颜色都照得一清二楚。那个农场主，对男孩这样死乞白赖地盯着看，似乎感到恼火，可是并没有赶他走，吩咐他让路，因此

1. 一码等于 0.914 米。（说明：书中脚注均为编者注。）

这个小小子一直走在他们前面。他的眼睛一直死盯着她，等到他们到达坡顶，农场主脸上露出放下心来的神情，撒开马小跑起来——从外表上看，不再注意那个男孩究竟怎样了。

“看那可怜的男孩盯着我看的那副神情！”年轻媳妇说。

“是呀，亲爱的，我看见他是在盯着你瞧。”

“他是村里的人吧，我猜？”

“是附近的一个人。我想他是和他妈住在一两英里[1]远的地方。”

“毫无疑问，他知道我们是谁吧？”

“啊，是的，你一定得预料到，刚开始人家会盯着你瞧，我漂亮的格楚德。”

“我料到了——不过我以为，这个可怜的男孩盯着我们瞧，可能是想让我们帮他带一下他背的那个沉重的大包，而不是出于好奇。”

“啊，不对，”她丈夫脱口而出，“这些乡下小子，只要东西一上肩，就可以背上一英担[2]，再说，他那个包看

---

1. 一英里等于 1.609 千米。

2. 一英担约等于 50.802 千克。

起来很大，实际上并不那么重。好啦，再走上一英里，我就可以远远地指给你看我们住的那所房子——要是我们赶到那儿天还不太黑的话。”车轮滚滚向前，又像以前那样把砂土碾得向四周乱迸，终于出现了一所占地阔大的白房子，房后还有一些专为干农活儿用的房子和干草堆。

这时候，那个男孩加快了脚步，在离这所白色农庄还有差不多一英里半的地方，拐到一条小路上，向着那些比较贫瘠的草场爬上去，一直走到他母亲的那所村舍。

她干完了她当天在外面奶场上挤奶的活儿，已经回到家里，正借着渐渐昏暗的光线，在门洞里洗菜。“把这个网兜拿一会儿。”男孩刚一走进来，她没有先打招呼就这样说。

他赶忙扔下他那个大包袱，抓住盛菜网兜的边，她一边往兜里放正在滴水的卷心菜，一边继续说话：“怎么样，你看见她了吗？”

“嗯，挺清楚的。”

“她像个太太吗？”

“嘿，不单像，还是个不折不扣的太太呢。”

“她年轻吗？”

“嗯，她已经是个大人啦。她那神气，十足是个女人。”

“当然。她的头发和脸蛋儿是什么颜色？”

“她头发是浅色的，脸蛋儿就像一个活的玩具娃娃。”

“她的眼睛，那么，不是像我的眼睛这样深颜色的吧？”

“不，是浅蓝色的，她的嘴长得挺俏挺红，笑起来露出一口白牙。”

“她个儿高吗？”她酸溜溜地问道。

“我看不见。她坐着呢。”

“那么，明天早晨你到霍姆斯托克教堂去，她准会去那儿。早点去，看着她走进去，回家来告诉我，她是不是比我高。”

“那好吧，妈妈。可是你干吗不自己去看看呢？”

“我去看她！她就是这会儿从我窗户前面走过去，我也不会抬头去看她。当然，她是和洛吉先生在一起。他说了些什么？做了些什么？”

“和平常一样。”

“没有注意你？”

“没有。”

第二天，母亲给孩子穿了一件干净的衬衫，打发他到霍姆斯托克教堂去。他到达这座小小的古老建筑的时候正赶上开门，他就第一个走了进去。他在洗礼盘旁边找了个座位，看着教区所有的教民鱼贯而入。阔气的农场主洛吉几乎是最后一个走进来的，伴随他的那个年轻的媳妇，走进教堂走廊，脸上带着羞涩的神情，这对于一个第一次在众人面前露面的端庄淑静的女人来说，也是自然而然的事。大家的目光都盯着她，所以这个年轻人的注视，现在也就没有引起人们的注意了。

他到达家门口的时候，还没等走进屋子，他母亲就问了:“怎么样？”

“她个儿并不高，还有点矮呢！”他回答说。

“啊！”他母亲满意地叫了一声。

“可是她很漂亮——很漂亮。说实话，她挺可爱。”自耕农的媳妇那种年轻鲜艳的神情，甚至给这个秉性多少有点严峻的男孩，显然留下了深刻的印象。

“这就是所有我想要听到的。”他母亲很快地说，“好啦，把桌布铺上。你用铁丝网套住的兔子很嫩，可是要小心，别让谁抓住你——你一直还没告诉我，她的手是什么样的。”

“我根本没见到。她一直没有脱下手套。”

“她今天早晨穿戴的什么？”

“一顶白帽子和一身银灰色的袍子。袍子蹭到教堂条凳上刺啦刺啦地响，声音那么大，那位太太自己听到这声音感到不好意思，脸红得比原先更厉害了，她把衣服拉起来，好让它别再蹭，可是她猛一下坐到位子上，那刺啦声更大了。洛吉先生，他好像很得意，他的背心露着，他那几颗金晃晃的大印吊着，就像一个大老爷似的，可是他太太好像是希望她那件闹人的袍子放在哪里都成，就是别穿在她身上。”

“是吗？不管怎么说，现在这就够啦！”

以后，这个男孩每次偶然碰见这对新婚夫妇，他母亲都要他陆续把他们的情况再讲一遍。若达·布茹克固然只要走上一两英里就可以很容易地亲自见到年轻的洛吉太太，但是她从没打算走这一点路，到农庄房舍所在的地方去。牛奶场的场院就在洛吉这远处的第二个农场里，她每天在场院挤奶的时候，也从来不提最近办的这桩婚事。牛奶场老板租了洛吉的奶牛，对这个高挑挤奶姑娘的身世也知道得清清楚楚，他怀着男子汉的善意，总是不让奶场场院里的这些流言蜚语引起若达苦恼。但

是洛吉太太到达以后最初那些日子，周围的环境老是充满这个话题。而若达·布茹克从她孩子的描述和其他挤奶工人偶尔露出的只言片语，也能够在心里描绘出对这个一无所知的洛吉太太的图像，就像照片那样逼真。

三　幻象

新人回家两三个星期后的一天晚上，男孩上床睡了，若达把泥煤灰扒出来放在面前，好让它们熄灭，她在那堆泥煤余火前面坐了很长时间。她就着那些余烬，按照她想象的模样，心里想着那个新媳妇，思考得那样聚精会神，竟忘记时间过去了多久，最后，由于一天工作的疲累，她也去睡觉了。

但是，这一天和前些天来一直萦回在她心中的形象，即使在夜晚也无法赶开。梦中，那个取代她的地位的格楚德·洛吉第一次来看她了。若达·布茹克在睡着以前确信自己真看见她了，而这是不足信的。她梦见这个年轻媳妇穿了一身浅灰色的衣服，戴着一顶白帽子，但是面容却歪歪扭扭，一塌糊涂，好像年纪很大，满脸皱纹。她躺在那儿，这个新媳妇就坐在她的胸脯上。洛吉太太

的身体压得越来越重，那双蓝眼睛冷酷无情地死盯着她的脸，然后这个影子又嘲弄地向前伸出左手，好让她戴的那个结婚戒指在若达的眼前熠熠闪耀。睡觉的人精神狂乱，给压得几乎透不过气来，她拼命挣扎。一会儿压在她身上的那个梦魔退到床脚去了，可是仍然死盯着她，随后又逐渐移上前来，重新坐在她胸脯上，又像刚才那样晃着左手。

若达使劲喘着气，最后拼命挣扎，抽出自己的右手，猛地抓住面前这个影子伸出的左臂，迅速把它向后拧着朝地上摔，她自己一下坐起来，同时发出一声低沉的叫喊。

“啊，善心的老天爷呀！”她叫喊着，坐在床边，出了一身冷汗。“这不是做梦——她到这儿来过了！”

甚至到这时候，她都能感觉到那只胳膊在她紧握的手掌中挣扎——好像真是有骨头有肉似的。她看看地上，她曾经把鬼影摔在那儿，但是地上什么也看不见。

若达·布茹克那天夜里再也没睡。第二天清早她去挤牛奶的时候，大家注意到，她的脸色惨白，显得疲乏不堪。她挤出的牛奶颤颤悠悠地流进牛奶桶，她的手到那时还没有平静下来，仍然感觉得到那只胳膊。她回家

吃早饭，就好像是到了吃晚饭的时候那样困。

“妈妈，昨天晚上你屋子里有声音，怎么啦？”她儿子问她，“你真从床上滚下来了吧？”

“你听见什么东西摔下来吗？什么时候？”

“刚好钟敲两点的时候。”

她无法解释，吃过早饭就一声不响地干起家务活儿来，男孩帮着她干，因为他讨厌到外面农场地里去，他不愿去，她也就惯着他。十一二点钟的时候，园子的门咔嚓一响，她抬头望着窗户，园子尽头门口站着她幻觉中的那个女人。若达好像一下子呆住了。

“啊，她说过她要来的！”男孩也看到了这个女人，大声喊着。

“这样说过——什么时候？她怎么知道我们？”

“我见过她，和她说过话。我昨天和她说过话。”

“我不是告诉过你了吗？”妈妈满脸通红愤怒地说，“不要和那所房子里的什么人说话，也不要走到那所房子跟前去。”

“我没和她说话，是她先和我说的。我也没有走到那所房子跟前，我在大路上碰到她的。”

“你告诉她什么啦？”

“什么也没有。她说：‘你就是那天从市场上背回那么重一包东西的那个可怜的孩子吗？’她看了看我的靴子，并且说，要是走在湿地上，这靴子没法儿让我的脚不湿，因为靴子都那么破了。我告诉她，我和妈妈一起过，我们为养活自己，已经做得够可以了，而且事实就是这样。那时候她就说了‘我给你带双好点的靴子来，并且看看你妈妈’。不光给我们，她还给牧场上别的人散东西呢。”

洛吉太太这时已经接近屋门口了——不是满身丝绸，像若达梦见在卧室里那样，而是戴了一顶晨帽，穿了一件普通薄料子的袍子，而这比丝绸更适合她。她胳膊上挎着一只篮子。

头天夜里所经历的事情，留下的印象仍然很强烈。布茹克差不多还以为可以从来访客人的脸上看到那些皱纹，那种蔑视，那种冷酷。如果能够躲开，她就会躲开，不和她见面。然而，这所房子并没有后门，洛吉太太轻轻一敲门，孩子就立刻把门闩拔开了。

“我说呢，我找这所房子是找对了。”她一边说，一边瞅了一眼这个小小子，满脸含笑，“可是不是你开门，我还没有把握呢。”

这种形象和举止同幻梦中的影子一模一样，但是她的声音那么难以言传的甜，她的一顾一盼都那么逗人喜欢，她的笑容那么温柔，完全不像若达夜半梦中那个来访的贵客，若达简直无法相信自己的感觉是否正确了。她本来因为非常讨厌而想一躲了事，这时她却真正感到高兴，她幸好没有躲开。洛吉太太篮子里带来了她原来答应给孩子的一双靴子，还有一些别的有用的东西。

面对这些说明洛吉太太对她和她的亲人亲切友善的感情，若达内心不觉在痛苦地责备自己。这个天真无辜的年轻人儿，应该得到她的祝福，而不是她的诅咒。她离开他们以后，屋子里好像少了一种光辉。两天以后，她又来了，想知道那双靴子是不是合脚；在那以后不到两个星期，她又来看了若达一次。这一次男孩不在家。

“我经常出来走走，”洛吉太太说，“你们的房子是我们自己那个教区以外离我们最近的了。我希望你身体很好。可是你看起来好像不太好。”

若达说她很好，的确，两个人比起来，她脸色比较苍白，可是她身体结实，身材高大，比起站在她面前的这位面容娇柔的年轻女人来，更有力量，更能耐劳。谈起谁强壮谁柔弱，谈话也就越来越亲密了。洛吉太太动

身离开的时候，若达说：“我希望这里的空气对你合适，太太，希望水浇牧场的潮气对你没有害处。”

年纪轻的这位回答说，这倒没有多大的问题，她总的健康状况通常都是很好的。“不过，你现在提醒我了，”她又接着说下去，“我有点小毛病，叫我闹不明白。它也并不是什么大不了的事，可是我就是弄不清楚。”

她露出她的左手和左胳膊，若达一看，就是她在梦中看见过并且猛地抓住的那只胳膊的样子。胳膊粉红圆润的表皮上，现出的淡淡的颜色带有病态的痕迹，像是给猛力抓住过而留下的手印。若达的眼睛死盯在这些变了颜色的痕迹上。在想象中，她以为她从中辨认出来了她的四根手指头的形状。

“这是怎么弄的？”她不动声色地问。

“我也说不上来，”洛吉太太一边摇头，一边说，“有一天晚上，我睡得很熟，梦见我去到一个有些陌生的地方，突然我的胳膊猛地一疼，疼得很厉害，把我疼醒了。我想，大概是我白天里撞了一下，可是我也记不得这样撞过。”她笑着又加了一句，“我对我亲爱的丈夫开玩笑说，看起来好像是他突然大发雷霆，在那儿打了我一下。噢，我敢说，它很快就会没了的。”

"哈，哈！是呀……那是哪一天夜里有的？"

洛吉太太想了想，然后说，那是两个星期以前的一个夜晚。"我醒过来的时候，记不清我到过哪里。"她又加了一句，"一直到钟敲了两点，这才提醒了我。"

她说出了若达与幻影相遇的那天夜晚和具体钟点，布茹克觉得好像成了一个罪人。这样没有一点矫饰虚夸就透露了真情，使她大为惊恐，但她并不把它设想为奇怪的巧合：闹鬼那天夜里的一切景象，都更加生动地重现在她心里了。

"啊，难道说，"客人走了以后，她自言自语道，"我能违反自己的意愿，对别人施加邪恶的力量吗？"她知道，她失身以后，有人一直偷偷地把她叫作女巫；但是她从来不明白，为什么要把这恶名加在她头上，不去管它也就过去了。难道这就是原因吗？难道像这样的事果真以前也发生过吗？

四　建议

夏天越来越近了，若达·布茹克几乎害怕再见到洛吉太太，尽管她对这个年轻的媳妇差不多可以说很有感

情了。若达个人品格上的某些东西似乎要把她自己判为有罪。然而出于命运安排，她有时离开家门不是为了上工，走着走着就走到霍姆斯托克附近去了；因此她们下一次会面也就到了户外。若达想避也避不开那个使她感到神秘的话题，说了不多几句话，她就吞吞吐吐地说："我想，你的——胳膊已经复原了吧，太太？"其实她早已惊愕地发现，格楚德·洛吉的左胳膊有些直挺挺的。

"不，还没怎么见好。说实在的，根本就没有见好，倒不如说是更坏了。有时候痛得要命。"

"也许你最好还是去找个医生看看，太太。"

她回答说，她已经找过医生了。她丈夫坚持要她去找一个医生。但是那位外科大夫好像根本不懂那只有病的胳膊是怎么回事。他告诉她用热水浸泡，她也泡过了，但是这种治疗一点用处也没有。

"让我看看，好吗？"挤奶妇问道。

洛吉太太把袖子卷上去，露出那个地方，就在手腕上边几英寸[1]。若达·布茹克一看见它，几乎都无法保持镇静了。那并不是像伤口一样的什么东西，但是胳膊上那个地方现出干瘪的样子，那四根手指头的轮廓比前一

1. 一英寸等于 0.025 米。

次显得更清楚了。不仅如此，她还想象出，这些指印刚好就在她恍惚之间使劲抓住的位置：第一根指头朝着格楚德的手腕，第四根指头朝向她的胳膊肘。

格楚德自己在她们上次会面之后，好像也感到这些印痕和什么相像。“看起来几乎就像手指印。”她说，接着淡淡一笑，“我丈夫说，好像是什么女巫，或者魔鬼抓住过我这个地方，把肌肉掐干瘪了。”

若达打了一个冷战。“那是胡思乱想，”她急忙说，“我要是你，我就不会在乎它。”

“我本来不应该那样在乎它，”年轻的那位迟迟疑疑地说，“要是……要是我没有一种感觉，觉得它使我丈夫……不喜欢我，不，不那样爱我。男人都那样喜欢考虑一个人的外表。”

“有些人是那样的——他就是一个。”

“是的，而且起先，他对我的外表非常得意。”

“把你的胳膊遮着，别让他瞧见。”

“唉——他知道那儿变样了！”她竭力想不让人看见她那满眼泪水。

“好了，太太，我真心诚意希望这事马上就过去。”

就这样，这个挤奶妇回家的时候，又重新让一种可

怕的魔力把自己的心同这件事情牢牢地拴在一起了。她装作嘲笑自己迷信，可是做了某种坏事的犯罪感还是增强了。若达在内心深处，并不完全反对她那位后任的花容月貌略微有点减损，不管是出于什么方式；但是也不希望使她遭受肉体上的痛苦，因为，虽然有了这个年轻漂亮的女人，洛吉再也不可能就他自己过去对若达的所作所为给予任何补偿，但是在这个较年长女人的心里，对别人完全出于无心的篡夺行为所怀有的任何愤恨，都早已烟消云散了。

如果这位甜美善良的格楚德·洛吉知道了卧房里的那场梦境，她会怎么想呢？和她保持友谊，而又不把这件事告诉她，好像就是不仁不义；但是她自己又不愿意主动地去告诉她——而且她也想不出什么补救的办法。

那天晚上她大部分时间都在思索这件事情。第二天，挤完了早晨那班牛奶之后，由于有一种可怕的魔力把她拉向洛吉太太那里，她就动身出去，想看看是不是能够再见格楚德·洛吉一面。挤奶姑娘从远处遥望那所房子，终于能够辨认出农场主的妻子独自一人骑马外出——大概是到远处的农场去和她丈夫会合。洛吉太太看见了她，就策马朝她这个方向慢慢跑来。

“早上好，若达！”格楚德跑过来的时候说，“我正要去看你呢。”

若达注意到，洛吉太太握住缰绳都有些困难。

“我希望——那只有毛病的胳膊……”若达说。

“他们告诉我，也许有一种办法，我可以找出它的原因，这样就可以把它治好，”另一位急匆匆地说，“那就是去找爱敦荒原上的一个什么聪明人。他们不知道他是否还活着——这会儿我一下想不起他的名字来了。但是他们说，你比附近不管谁都更了解他的动静，可以告诉我，是不是还可以找他请教。哎呀——他叫什么名字？你是知道的。”

“不是纯德法师吗？”她问着，瘦削的脸变得惨白了。

“纯德——对了。他还活着吗？”

“我相信他还活着。”若达勉勉强强地说。

“你为什么把他称作法师？”

“嗯——他们说……他们一直说，他是个……他有许多别人没有的能力。”

“唉，我们那些人怎么那样迷信，要介绍这种人？我原来以为他们说的是个什么行医的人呢。我不想再找

他了。”

若达看来松了一口气，洛吉太太骑马走了。挤奶妇听说别人提出向她打听这个人，那时，她就从内心感到，工友中间一定有某种讥讽的看法，说一个女巫会知道那个魔法师的下落。那么，他们是在怀疑她。不久以前，这种事不会让她这个明理的女人在意。但是，现在她可有一个挥之不去让她迷信的理由了。她突然恐惧起来，害怕这个法师会指名道姓，说她是那个正在摧毁格楚德美貌的恶人，因而使她那位朋友永远恨她，把她看成是化作人形的魔鬼。

但是所有一切都还没有完结。过了两天，午后的太阳透过窗格子照进来，在若达·布茹克家的地上投下了一个黑影。这个女人立刻开了门，几乎都喘不过气来了。

“你一个人在家吗？”格楚德问道。她看来也同若达·布茹克本人一样焦虑急躁。

“是。”若达说。

“我胳膊上那块地方看来好像更糟了，这让我很苦恼！”这个年轻的农场主太太继续说，“它多么奇怪呀！我真希望它不会是一种不治之症。我一直又在考虑他们所说的纯德法师的事。我并不真信那种人，但是我觉得，

只是去看看他并不碍事，出于好奇吧——不过绝不应该让我丈夫知道。到他住的地方去远吗？”

“是——有五英里地呢，”若达迟迟疑疑地说，“在爱敦荒原最里边。”

“嗯，我应该步行去。你能和我一起去，帮我带带路吗？——比如说，明天下午？”

“啊，我不行。那是——”挤奶妇低声咕哝着，心中一惊。她突然觉得很恐惧，害怕她在梦中采取那种猛烈行动的事会泄露出来，那样，在她这个平生最有益的朋友眼中，她的人格就完了，而且再也无可挽回了。

洛吉太太一再撺掇，若达虽然非常担心，最后还是同意了。这条道路对她说来固然很伤心，可是她的恩人那种奇怪的病有可能治好，她就不能蓄意挡她的道。最后两人商量好，为了避免别人对她们这种不可思议的意图产生怀疑，她们决定在荒原边沿一块人工林的角落上会合。从她们现在站着的地方就可以看见那个角落。

五　纯德法师

在第二天下午以前，若达本来可以做出一些事情来

逃避这次探访，但是她已经答应了要去。不仅如此，如果真能有助于找到一种可能的方法，弄清究竟，也许可以发现她在那个神秘莫测的世界里还是一个人物，比她过去对她自己设想过的更加了不起，这本身有时就具有一种可怕的诱惑力。

快到她们约定的那个时间，她出发了，经过半小时轻快的步行，她走到了这一地带爱敦荒原的东南边缘，那里有一片枞树林。一个身材娇小的人，穿着外套，戴着面罩，早已到了那里。若达一看到洛吉太太用吊带把左胳膊吊着，几乎浑身打了一个哆嗦。

她们彼此几乎没有讲什么话，就立即开始爬坡，朝这片森严肃穆的荒野深处走去。这片地方居高临下，俯视她们半小时之前刚刚离开的那片冲积而成的富饶土地。这是一次长途跋涉。乌云使整个环境显得阴暗，虽然这时还不过刚到下午。风在荒原的斜坡上凄厉地嚎叫，这个荒原未必就不是那个目睹过威塞克斯国王伊那的痛苦的荒原，而后世则把伊那描述为李尔[1]。格楚德·洛吉说话

1. 英国历史家兼博古家凯姆敦（1551—1623），在他的《不列颠纪拾遗》里，曾提过威塞克斯的国王是伊那，哈代以此为据，引用到自己的书中。但除此以外，包括莎士比亚在内的其他大家作品中，所提到的威塞克斯国王均为李尔。

多，若达只是用简单几个现成的字眼儿回答。她有一种奇怪的厌恶心理，不愿走在这个同伴吊着那条有毛病的胳膊的那一边，一不小心靠近那条胳膊了，她就转身走到另一边去。下坡走向一条车道的时候，她们的脚扫着了许多石楠。她们要寻找的那个人的房子就在路旁。

他并不承认他开业治病，或者关心与此相关的任何事情。他直接关心的是经营常青棘、泥煤、“粗砂”等土特产品。的确，他假装并不相信自己的能力，人们请他治疗瘊子，这些瘊子奇迹般地消失了——必须承认，的确是消失了——他会轻描淡写地说：“噢，我不过是对着那些瘊子喝了杯烈酒，也许是凑巧了吧。”而且马上就转换话题。

她们到达的时候，他正好在家，事实上是看着她们下到他这个山谷里来的。他胡须灰白，脸色红润。他一见到若达，就用一种奇特的眼神盯着她。洛吉太太告诉他，她是来干什么的。他一边嘴里叨唠着自己不行，一边又检查她的胳膊。

“药可治不了它，”他立刻说，“这是一个仇人干的。”

若达缩作一团，倒退了两步。

“一个仇人？什么仇人？”洛吉太太问道。

他摇摇头。“那你自己最容易弄清楚，”他说，“要是你愿意，我可以把那个人给你指出来。不过我自己并不会知道那是谁。别的我干不了，也不想干。”

她催着他干。于是他告诉若达，让她在外面她现在站的地方等着，然后把洛吉太太领进屋里。屋门马上开了，而且后来一直留着一道缝儿，因此若达没有跟他们在一起，也可以看见他们自始至终在干些什么。他从食具柜里拿出一只平底酒杯，装上大半杯水，并且拿出一个鸡蛋，用某种不让别人知道的办法摆弄了一番，然后就着玻璃杯的边缘把蛋敲破，让蛋清流进去，蛋黄留在蛋壳里。因为天越来越暗了，他就把酒杯和酒杯里的东西一起拿到窗前，告诉格楚德仔细地观察水里的东西。他们俩一起躬身靠近桌子，挤奶妇能够看见蛋清在水里下沉的时候形状不断变化泛起的乳白色，但是她离得不够近，看不出它成了什么形状。

“你看的时候，能够看得出像什么人的脸或者模样吗？”法师对年轻的女人说。

她小声回答，声音轻得若达听不见，并且还继续全神贯注地看着杯子里面。若达转过身去，向远处走了几步。

洛吉太太出来了，阳光照在她脸上，在荒原景物忧郁暗淡的色调衬托之下，她的脸显得特别惨白——和若达的脸一样惨白。纯德在她走出之后把门关上了，她们立刻一起回家。但是若达看得出来，她的同伴完全变了。

“他收费很多吗？”她探问道。

“啊，不——没花钱。他分文不取。”格楚德说。

“那么，你看到什么啦？”若达问道。

“什么……什么我也不乐意说。”她那种小心谨慎的样子很明显。她的脸板着，一下变老了，有点像若达卧室中的那张脸。

“是你首先建议到这里来的吗？”洛吉太太停了很久以后突然问道，“如果是你首先建议的，那该多怪呀！”

“不是。但是就目前的情况来看，我并不认为这个决定是错误的。”她回答道。她忽然第一次有了一种胜利感，她一点也不悔恨，她身边的这个小东西该知道，并不是她们自己，而是别的什么有影响力的东西，使她们不相容。

在回家去的这条漫长而又累人的路上，再也没有人提到这个话题了。但是，那年冬天在那片有很多牛奶场的低地上，以这种或那种方式悄悄流传着这样一个故事:

洛吉太太的左胳膊慢慢不中用了，是因为若达·布茹克用“目光震慑”住了。若达对于那场梦魇保有她自己的想法，但是她的面容越来越愁苦，越来越消瘦。到了春天在霍姆斯托克附近就再也见不到她和她那个男孩了。

六　第二次尝试

六年过去了，洛吉先生和太太的婚后生活平淡乏味，而且更糟。农场主常常闷闷不乐，沉默寡言；而那个女人，以前由于优雅和美貌而受到他的热烈追求，这时左臂已经变形，不成样子。不仅如此，她也并没有给他生孩子，这就大有可能使他在大约二百年来占有这个河谷的家族中，成为末代子孙了。他想起若达·布茹克和她的儿子，害怕这可能就是上天对他的判决。

过去一向心情轻快、头脑开明的格楚德，逐渐变成了一个容易激动、思想迷信的女人，她全部时间都用来为治她的病痛做试验，采用她碰上的任何一个江湖医生的药方。她一心眷恋丈夫，还暗怀着痴心妄想至少挽回她身上原有的某些美貌，来赢得他的回心转意，因此她的私室里摆满了各式各样的瓶瓶、包包、药盒、药

罐——不仅这些，还有一包包神秘的草药、种种符咒和宣讲巫术的书籍，要是在她的学生时代，她一定会嘲笑说这些东西都是愚蠢胡闹。

“见鬼。看吧，这些药店乱配的杂烩和巫婆胡掺和的东西，哪一天不把你自己毒死才怪呢。”她丈夫偶尔看到那一排又一排的玩意儿就这样说。

她并不回答，只是用那样一种痛心的责备神情，向他投去悲哀而又温情的一瞥，所以他显出对自己的话感到歉意的样子，又加了一句:“你知道，我这不过是为了你好，格楚德。”

“我要把这些劳什子一股脑儿都清理出来，全部毁掉，”她哑着嗓子说，“再也不试那种药方了！”

“你得有个什么人，让你高兴起来。”他说，“我曾经想抱养一个男孩，可是他现在岁数太大了，而且他走了，我也不知道现在他在什么地方。”

她猜到了他指的是谁，因为这些年来，若达·布茹克的事她已经知道了，虽然她丈夫从来没有就这件事和她交谈过一个字。她也从来没有对他说过，她曾经去拜访过纯德法师，也没说过那个孤零零地住在荒原上的人给她透露过什么，或者她以为给她透露过什么。

她现在二十五岁，但是看起来要老得多。“六年的婚姻，不过几个月的爱情。”有时她这样自言自语。于是她想到那个显而易见的原因，看看自己那条日益萎缩的胳膊，满怀悲哀地说：“要是我能够再变回原来的模样，就像他第一次见到过的那样，那该多好呀！”

她顺从地毁掉了那些丹方符咒，但是仍然保留着一种热切的愿望，想试试另外的东西——完全不同的另一种疗法。自从若达勉为其难地领着她去拜访过那位离群索居的人以后，她再也没有重访纯德。但格楚德现在突然想起，她可以再做孤注一掷的努力，来消除这种看来像是受到诅咒的灾祸，如果他还活着，就再去找找他。他应该是可信的，因为他在酒杯中造出的那个不大清晰的形象，毫无疑问是和一个女人相像，虽然那时她还不知道，可是她现在知道了，世界上只有那个女人有理由对她不怀好意。是应该再去拜访一次。

这一次她是一个人去的，不过她在荒原上几乎迷了路，比她应该走的路多绕了很远的一段。然而，最后总算到了纯德的那所房子，他不在家，没有在屋子里等她。远处他那伛偻的身影，指明他在那个地方干活儿，她走了过去。纯德还记得她。他把他收集的常青棘根放下，

堆成一堆，提出要陪着她朝她回家的路上走走，因为路程很远，而白天又很短。这样他们就一起走着，他的头低得几乎都要触到地面了，而且他的外表和地面是一个颜色。

“我知道，你可以把瘊子、瘤子消掉，”她说，“为什么不能把这个消掉呢？”她说着就露出了胳膊。

“你把我的力量想得太大了！”纯德说，“我现在是年纪又老，身体又弱。不行，不行。我亲自干，干不了。你试过些什么办法？”

她时时变换，用过上百种治病的药物和驱邪的符咒，她给他举出了几种，他摇了摇头。

“有一些是够好的，”他用赞成的口气说，“可是其中有许多并非如此。这种病是一种萎缩性的，不是创伤性的，而且只要你一下把它摆脱了，那马上就会完全好了。”

“要是我能那样该多好！”

“我所知道的，只有唯一一种机遇能行。治疗类似的病痛，这个办法从来没有不灵的——我敢这样说。不过做起来难，特别是一个女人。”

“告诉我吧！”她说。

“你必须用那条胳膊去摸上过绞刑的人的脖子。”

他讲的这种景象把她吓了一跳。

“要在刚从绞刑架上放下来尸体还没有冰凉的时候。”法师不动声色地继续说。

“那样做有什么好处呢？”

“它可以调理血脉，改变体质。不过，我刚说过，做起来很难。你得在有绞刑的时候到监狱去，在那里等着把人从绞刑架上放下来，好多人都那样干过，不过也许没有像你这样漂亮的女人。我一向打发皮肤有毛病的人去，总有几十人了。不过，那都是以前的事，我打发去的最后一个人，是在一八一三年——都差不多有十二年啦。”

他再没有对她说什么，然后把她送上一条回家去的直路，就转身离开了她，和第一次一样，一文钱也不肯收。

七 骑马赶路

这番话深深地印在格楚德的心里了。她的性格属于有点怯弱的那种，大概这个善心的术士所能够推荐的一

切疗法中，没有任何一种能像这种办法那样，使她充满反感，更不用说实行起来会遇到的不计其数的障碍了。

到郡城所在地卡斯特桥有十二英里或十五英里。虽然在那个犯盗马罪、纵火罪、夜盗罪的人都要处死刑的年月，一场巡回审判过后很少有不判绞刑的，但是，没有别人帮忙，她大概没法儿接近犯人的尸体。而她又害怕她丈夫会大发雷霆，所以不愿意把纯德的建议向他或他周围的人透露一个字。

她等了几个月，什么也没做，只是像以前一样，耐心地忍受着破相的痛苦。但是，她毕竟是一个女人，从天性来说，总想恢复自己的秀美姿容，重新得到爱情（她还不过二十五岁呀），这种渴望不断地刺激她，要她尝试一下这种无论如何也不大可能使她受到任何伤害的办法。“用魔法降临的，也一定得用魔法赶走。”她常这样说。可是她的想象里一出现这种行动，她就恐惧退缩，不敢正视这种可能性。随后，法师讲的“它可以调理血脉”这句话又来了，好像它能够变成一种符合科学的解释，而不是一派胡言乱语。同时那种难以抑制的想克服病痛的愿望也催促她再去尝试尝试。

那个时候，郡里只有一家报纸，她丈夫也只是偶尔

借阅一下。但是过去也有过去的办法。人们广泛用口舌传递消息，从一个市场到另一个市场，从一个集市到另一个集市，所以一有执行死刑这类事情快要发生，方圆二十英里之内，几乎没有人不知道这种马上要来的光景，哪怕远在霍姆斯托克，也有些热心的人，据大家所知道的，步行去到卡斯特桥，一天之内走个来回，就是为了亲眼看看那场热闹。下一次巡回审判定在三月；格楚德·洛吉听说审判已经举行了，一找到机会就偷偷地向酒馆、客店打听审判的结果。

然而，她已经太迟了。行刑的时间已经到了，走那么一段路，还要在那样短的时间内就能获准进去，那至少要得到她丈夫的帮助。她可不敢告诉他，因为她刚稍微一试探就已经发现，农村中此类迷信的念头，只要一提就使他火冒三丈，一半原因是他自己对这类念头也半信半疑，因此她只好再等另一次机会。

她听说，就在霍姆斯托克的这个村子里，多年以前有两个患癫痫病的孩子曾经去过，而且效果很好，尽管附近的教会人士强烈谴责这种做法，这种事情还是使她的决心得到鼓舞。四月、五月、六月都过去了，可以毫不夸张地说，到了六月底的时候，格楚德简直是在热切

希望把什么人处死了。她平时每天晚上都做常规的祈祷，这时她却不知不觉地这样祈祷起来了：“啊，上帝，快把一个什么人绞死吧，管他有罪还是无辜！”

这一次她更早就开始打听，她的做法也更加按部就班。不仅如此，当时正是夏季，处在储草和收获之间，她丈夫有空闲时间，常常离家在外度假。

巡回审判是在七月份，她又像以前那样到客店去打听。只判了一个死刑——仅仅一个——罪名是纵火。

她最大的问题倒不是如何去卡斯特桥，而是采用什么办法可以获准进入监狱。虽然为了这种目的而提出进入监狱，这种申请以前从来没有遭到过拒绝，可是这种习俗现在已经不时兴了。她考虑到可能遇到的困难，差不多又要迫不得已回过头来去依靠她丈夫了。但是，她对巡回审判的事情稍微一试探，他就显得那么不愿谈论，甚至比以前更加冷淡，所以她没往下再说，决定不管要做什么，她都自己一个人去做。

一向冷酷无情的命运，于她来说出乎意料地好转了。死刑定在星期六，星期四的时候，洛吉先生对她说，他要再离家一两天，到集市上去做点生意，并且说他很抱歉，不能带她一起去。

这次她表示非常乐意留在家里，这使他感到惊讶，盯着她直看。她以前对于失去这种短途旅游的机会，总是表现出强烈失望的。然而，他慢慢恢复了他一向沉默寡言的态度，到了所说的那一天，就离开了霍姆斯托克。

现在该轮到她了。她最初想赶车去，可是仔细一想，又打住了，因为那样她就得走税卡路，她那鬼鬼祟祟的使命让人发觉的可能性就要增加十倍了。本来在结婚之前，她丈夫答应过要经常留一匹牝马供她骑用，而这时在她丈夫的几个马厩里，无论想象多么出格，也找不到一匹适合女人的坐骑；尽管如此，她还是决心骑马，并且避开人们常走的路。她丈夫有许多拉车的马，很好的驭马，留下的马匹中间有一匹可以使唤。这是一匹体形高大的亚马逊牝马，马背宽得像一只沙发，她小有不适的时候，偶尔也骑出去换换空气。她挑上了这匹马。

星期五下午，一个伙计把它溜熟了。她已经穿戴停当，临走前她看着那条干瘪的胳膊。“哎呀！”她说，“如果不是为了你，我就不会去受这一趟可怕的罪啦！”

她带了几件衣物，打了一个小包，趁这个机会对仆人说：“我去看一个朋友，怕今天晚上回不来，所以带了这些东西。要是我十点钟还没回来，不要惊慌，像平日

一样把家门关好。明天我肯定会回来。”她打算以后再私下告诉她丈夫，做完了的事不像计划要做的事，他差不多肯定会宽恕她的。

于是，这个颇为忐忑的格楚德·洛吉离开了丈夫的宅院。但是，尽管她的目的地是卡斯特桥，她却没有走直路经过斯蒂克福到那里去。她耍花招最初走的路刚好是相反的方向。然而，她一走到人们看不见她的地方，就向左拐，走上去爱敦荒原的路。刚要走上荒原的时候，又拐一个弯，走上真正要走的路，向正西方走去。很难想象出，到郡城去还有比这更隐秘的路了；至于方向，她只需要把马头牢牢对准太阳右边一点就行。她懂得，她随时可以碰到砍常青棘的或者村舍里的什么人，问问他们就不会走错了路。

虽然说来那时离现在还不太久远，可是爱敦远远不像现在这个样子把地面都分成了小块小块的，人们想在低坡上开垦，不管结果是成功还是失败，都把原来的荒原分割成了许多互不相连的小荒原。而那时候，这些还不太盛行，还没实现圈地法，田埂和树篱都还没建立起来。不像现在这样：村民的牲口不能享有从前在公有地上放牧的权利，那些享有泥煤开采特权的人自己的大车

也不能随便到处走，保证他们一年到头都有东西烧。因此格楚德骑马走去，除了带刺的常青棘丛、一片片石楠、白色的水沟、地表上自然的悬崖和斜坡以外，并没有别的什么障碍。

她那匹马如果大踏步、慢慢走很稳当，虽然是一匹挽马，走得却从容不迫。如果不是这样，她就不敢端着一条半死不活的胳膊，骑上它走这样一片村野荒地了。因此，她快要离开荒原下到满是耕地的山谷之前，走到了荒原通向卡斯特桥的路上最后一块边远的高地，勒住缰绳让她的坐骑喘口气，这时候，已经快到八点钟了。

她停在一个叫作灯草池的水塘边，池子两侧是两道树篱的尽头，一道栏杆通过池子中心，把水池分为两半。从栏杆上面望过去，是乡间的低绿地，越过绿树，是市镇的房项，越过房顶有一道房子平平的白色前脸儿，那就是郡监狱的入口。这道房子前脸儿的房顶上，有几个小黑点在来回挪动；看来他们像是几个工人在竖一个什么东西。她觉得毛骨悚然。她缓慢地往下走，不久就走到玉米地和牧场中间了。又过了半小时以后，格楚德走到城市这一边的第一个客店白鹿客栈，这时差不多已是暮色苍茫了。

她到达这里并没有激起什么人的惊讶。那个年月，农夫的妻子骑马赶路，比现在要多，不过，此情此景别人也根本想象不出洛吉太太已经身为人妻了。客栈老板以为她是一个轻率莽撞的年轻女人，到这里来看第二天的“绞刑盛会”。她丈夫和她本人都没有在卡斯特桥市场上做过买卖，所以没有人认识她。下马的时候她看到一群男孩就在客栈前面围在一个马具店的大门口，兴趣盎然地在朝里面看。

“那儿在干什么？”她问客栈的马夫。

“搓绳子明天好用。”

她会意地心头一悸，并且把胳膊缩回来了。

“事情完了以后，这根绳子要一寸一寸地卖，”那个马夫接着说，“要是你想要，小姐，我可以给你弄一段，免费的。”

她赶紧打消了任何这类念头，主要是因为她不知道怎么忽然有了一种奇怪的感觉，好像那个判了死刑的可怜人的命运，和她自己的命运交织在一起了。她订了一个房间准备过夜，然后坐下寻思。

究竟应该用什么办法获得允许进入监狱，一直到现在她连哪怕是最模糊的一点主意也没有。她忽然想起那

个神通广大的人说过的那番话。他曾经暗示过，她可以利用她的美貌——尽管遭到了损害，作为通关的钥匙。她没有经验，狱卒、狱吏她都不认识。她曾经听说过一个郡长和副郡长，但是也只是模糊地提到。然而她知道，一定有一个绞刑吏，于是她决定去求绞刑吏。

八　水边隐士

在那个年月以及几年以后，几乎每个监狱都有一个绞刑吏。格楚德经过打听才知道，卡斯特桥的那个小吏住在悬崖下面那条很深、很缓的河流旁边一个孤零零的村舍里，悬崖上面就是监狱那些房子的所在。而那条河，虽然她并不知道，就是灌溉下游斯蒂克福德和霍姆斯托克那一带草场的同一条河。

格楚德换了衣服，没吃没喝就出发了，因为不把某些具体事情定下来，她就是无法让自己安下心来。她沿着河边的一条小路走向所说的那所房子。走过监狱附近，在天空的映衬下，可以看得出来，在门道上面的平房顶上，有三个长方形的框子，她远远望去，有几个黑影在那里活动，她认出了竖起的东西是什么，于是快步走过

去。再走了一百码，她就到了行刑人的房子，这是一个男孩指给她的。房子就在同一条河流的旁边，紧靠一座排闸，河水流过不断发出轰隆的声响。

她站在那儿犹豫不决，这时门开了，一个老人走了出来，用一只手遮住一根蜡烛。他从外面把门锁上，转身登上一座木踏板楼梯，楼梯安在那所房子的边上，他开始上楼，显然这是通往他卧室的楼梯。格楚德赶忙上前，但是等赶到楼梯下面，他已经上到楼梯顶上了。她朝着他高声叫喊，声音足可以盖过排闸那边的轰鸣，让他听见，他往下看着问道:“你来这儿干啥？”

“和你说一分钟。”

烛光总算还照在了她仰面朝上颜色惨白而且带着乞求神情的脸上，戴维斯（大家都这样称呼这个绞刑吏）又走下楼梯。“我正要睡觉去了，”他说，“‘早睡早起’嘛，可是为了像你这样的一位女士，耽搁一分钟我是不会在乎的。进屋里来吧。”他重新打开门，把她领到屋子里面。

他平常干活的工具，也就是短工花匠的工具，摆在墙角，他大概看出了她像个乡下人，于是说道:“要是你想找我去干乡下的活儿，我可不能去，因为我从来没有

离开过卡斯特桥，为高贵的或是低微的人去干事儿——别找我吧。尽管有的时候我会让别人“离开”这里。”他正式地加了一句。

“是呀，是！是那样。明天！”

“啊，我想是这么回事。好吧，那又怎么样啦？关于绳结的事，到这儿来没有用——人们不断到这儿来，可是俺告诉他们，这个结也好，那个结也好，只要你把它打在耳朵下面，都是一样仁慈的。那个不幸的又是个亲戚吗？或者我该说，也许是（他看了看她的装束）你雇用的一个人？”

“不是。绞刑在什么时候执行？”

“和以前一样——十二点，或者说只等伦敦来的邮车一到就执行。我们总是等邮车到，准备等缓刑令。”

“噢——缓刑令——我希望没有！”她不觉说了出来。

“好吧——嘻——嘻！——当作公事办，我也这么希望！可是不管怎样，如果说一个年轻小伙子应该得到从轻发落的话，这个小伙子就应该。才刚刚十八岁出头嘛，而且只是碰巧在草垛着火的时候在那儿。不管怎么说，那并没有多大的危险，其实他们是不得已拿他来杀一儆百，这些日子像那样破坏财产的事太多啦。”

“我的意思是，”她解释说，“我想摸摸他，作为治病的法术，治一种病痛。有一个人证明，这种疗法很灵，是他出的主意。”

“噢，是的，小姐！现在我懂了。前几年有这种人来找过我。可是我想不到，你会是需要调理血脉的那种人。是怎么不好？这种事搞错了，我可担着责任呢。”

“我的胳膊。”她很不情愿地露出那块干瘪的皮肤来。

“啊，这就是胳膊萎缩！”绞刑吏一边观察一边说。

“是。”她说。

“好吧，”他很感兴趣地接着说，“我不得不承认，这真是个很好的病例！我喜欢这种样子的伤，就我所见过的来比较，这肯定真正适合做这种治疗。告诉你来这儿的，不管他是谁，可真是一个明白人。”

“你能费心帮我把要办的都安排好吗？”她屏住呼吸问。

“你应该去找监狱长，和你的医生一起去，说出你的名字和住址——要是我记得不错，一向都是这么办的。不过，也许俺能帮你办，只要很少一点费用。”

“噢，谢谢你！我宁愿这么办，因为我愿意保密。”

“不让情人知道，嗯？”

“不是，是不让丈夫知道。”

“哈哈！好极了。俺会让你摸一下尸体。”

“它现在在哪儿？”她一边说一边颤抖。

“它？你的意思是说他吧，他现在还活着。在上面那个暗处，就在那个小矮窗后面。”他指着悬崖上面的那个监狱。

她想起她丈夫和她那些朋友。“是的，当然啰，”她说，“那么，我怎么进行呢？”

他把她领到门口。“看，你可以等在那堵墙上的小门旁边，你往上走，在那个小巷里就可以找到，不要迟过一点钟。我从里边把门打开，因为不把他放下来，我是不会回家吃饭的。晚安。要准时到；要是你不想让别人看见你，罩块面纱。嗯——俺有一阵子有过你这么个女儿！”

她走了，爬上上面的那条小路，想自己先去弄清楚，好在第二天能够找到那扇小门。小门的轮廓，她很快就看得见了——是在监狱外面围墙上的一个小缺口。这是那么高的一个陡坡，她爬到小门旁边，不得不停下喘一会儿气，她朝后面望了一下水边的那所小房子，看见绞刑吏又在爬他户外的楼梯。他进了楼梯顶上的那个阁楼，

或者屋子，过了几分钟，他的烛光就灭了。

郡城的钟敲了十点，她像她刚到的时候那样，回到了白鹿客栈。

九　不期而遇

星期六中午一点钟。格楚德·洛吉像前面说过的那样，得到允许进入监狱，坐在第二道大门里面一个会客室里。这道门建在条石砌成的古典式拱廊下面，在当时看来，拱廊还是比较新式的，门上有几个字："郡监狱；1793 年"。这就是她前一天从荒原上看到的那面墙。旁边有一个通道，通向竖着绞刑架的房顶。

城里面人山人海，市场暂时停业了，但是格楚德几乎没有见到一个人影，她在屋子里一直待到约定的时刻，然后就动身去指定的地点。她走的那条路避开了悬崖下面那片开阔地带，观众那时都会集在那里，但是她甚至能听得见那里人声鼎沸。喧嚣声停顿的时候，一个沙哑的粗嗓子大叫了一声："死前最后遗言，忏悔！"并没来缓刑令，绞刑已经执行了；但是大伙还在等着，想看看尸体怎样卸下来。

不久，这个苦苦等待的女人听到头顶上有脚步声，然后就有一只手招呼她，她随着指引的方向，走了出去，穿过门房外面铺平了的院子。她的双膝发抖，简直走不动了。她一只胳膊露在袖子外面，只用披肩盖着。

她现在来到的地方，有两个支架，她还没来得及想这两个支架是干什么用的，就听见沉重的脚步在她背后什么地方下楼。她没有转过头去，或者无法转过头去，就用这种姿势僵在那里：她模模糊糊感到有四个人抬着一个粗糙的棺材和她擦肩而过。棺材敞开着，里面躺着一个年轻小伙子的尸体，身上穿着一件农民干活儿穿的长罩衫和一条粗斜纹布过膝短裤。尸体是匆匆忙忙扔进棺材的，所以罩衫的下摆吊在上面。这副沉重的东西暂时搁在支架上。

这个年轻女人现在处于这样一种状态：好像有一阵灰色的雾在她眼前浮动，因为这个缘故，再加上她又戴着面纱，她简直分辨不出任何东西，她好像已经快要死了，只是由于某种电流刺激才缓着没有断气。

“来吧！”紧靠她身边有个声音，她刚刚能意识到，这句话是对她说的。

她拼命使出最后的一点气力，向前走去，就在这个

时候，她听见背后有人向她走过来。她露出她那只被诅咒的可怜的胳膊，于是戴维斯揭开罩在尸体脸上的布，拉过格楚德的手举着，好让她的胳膊搭在死者的脖子周围，像还没熟透的黑莓果那种颜色的一道线上面。

格楚德尖叫了一声:法师预言的“调理血脉”实现了。但是就在这个当口，第二声尖叫响彻这个围墙里面的整个空间，它不是格楚德的喊叫。这一声尖叫使她大吃一惊，不禁往四处看。

紧靠她身后，站着若达·布茹克，她的脸歪扭着，两只眼睛因为哭泣而红肿起来了。若达身后站着格楚德自己的丈夫，他的脸上布满皱纹，两眼黯然无光，但是并没有眼泪。

“见鬼！你来这里干什么？”他声音沙哑地问道。

“臭婊子——现在到我们和我们孩子中间来了！”若达大叫，“这就是魔鬼在幻梦中显示给我的意思！到头来你还是像她！”她一把抓住这个年轻女人袒露出来的那只胳膊，把她死命地向后拉，一直把她顶到墙上。布茹克刚一松手，年轻虚弱的格楚德就滑溜下来，瘫靠在她丈夫的脚上，他把她抱起来的时候，她已经不省人事了。

一看见那一对，就足以提醒她，死去的年轻人是若

达的儿子。在那个时代，罪犯处死之后，他的亲属只要愿意就有权要求领回尸体下葬，因此洛吉同若达一起在等待验尸。这个年轻人这次被拘留之后，若达就把他叫去了，以后又在不同的时候叫去过几次，而且审判期间，他还曾经在法庭出席。这就是他近来经常沉迷其中的“度假”。这一对可怜的父母原来希望避免事情暴露，因此他们亲自来收尸，运尸的马车和盖尸的单子都在外面等着呢。

格楚德的病情十分严重，所以大家认为最好还是让她在附近就医。她被抬出监狱送往市内，但是她再也没有活着回家。她脆弱的生命力，由于胳膊瘫痪也许一直在逐渐给榨干，而在这以前的二十四小时内，她的身体和精神方面都受到重压，于是一受到双重的震惊就彻底垮了。她的血脉的确得到了“调理”——但是太过头了。两天以后，她就在市内死去。

她的丈夫再也没有在卡斯特桥露过面，仅仅在他一向经常光顾的安格伯瑞老市场曾经露过一次面。而在任何公开场合，他都很少出现。他最初由于郁郁寡欢和悔恨交加，心情沉重，后来逐渐好转，看来像是一个历经磨炼和细心体贴的人了。他参加了他那年轻亡妻的葬礼之后，立即采取了放弃霍姆斯托克和邻近教区的农场的

行动，并且卖掉了他的每一头牲口，然后离开，去到这个郡另一头的波特布瑞迪，住在那里孤零零的寓所中，直到两年以后因衰竭无疾而终。直到那个时候，大家才知道，他早已把他那笔不算菲薄的财产，全部遗赠给一家男童感化院，唯一的附带条件是，如果能找到若达·布茹克认领，就给她一小笔年金。

有一段时间，并没有找到她。但是她终于在她那个老教区重新出现了，不过她坚决拒绝与为她制定的规定有什么瓜葛。她又恢复了在牛奶场挤奶那种毫无变化的活儿，一直干了很多年，直到最后身体变得伛偻了，原来那一头浓密的头发变成了银丝，前额也脱光了——也许是因为挤奶时长期顶着奶牛的缘故。这里一些了解她身世的人，有时会站住看着她，并且寻思：随着那交错流下的条条奶流的节奏，在那个一动不动、满布皱纹的脑门儿后面，有些什么阴沉忧郁的思想在那儿悸动呢？

（张扬　张玲　译）

止不住打喷嚏的贼

很多很多年前，当现在已不茂盛的老橡树还只和老绅士的拐杖一样粗的时候，有位农民和儿子住在韦塞克斯。当时儿子休伯特十四岁上下，直率坦荡又英勇果敢，大家都很看好他。不过这个小伙子倒是有一点自负。

一个寒冷的圣诞节前夜，由于人手不足，父亲只能差遣他去离家数英里外的小镇办个重要差事。他是骑马去的，又被差事拖到很晚，时间已近深夜。所幸最后事情圆满解决了，他赶回小旅馆，给马配好鞍后，就上路了。回家要穿过肥沃但有些荒僻的布莱克摩山谷，那时的山谷土质黏重，小路蜿蜒，和如今一样被大片丛林所覆盖。

大约九点前后，休伯特骑着自己壮实的矮脚马杰瑞，

走在遮天的林荫小道上，哼起了圣诞颂歌。仿佛是为了应和此情此景，他恍惚觉得自己听到林间有些微响动，不由得想起，他所经过的这个地方可是恶名在外，以前路过的人曾在此遭到伏击。休伯特看看杰瑞，真希望它不是这一身亮灰鬃毛，其他任何颜色都好；因为如此一来，即便在昏暗的荫蔽中，这匹温驯小马的身形也清晰可见。“我在担心什么呢？”他想了一下，大声说道，“杰瑞这么敏捷矫健，一定不会让强盗靠近我的。”

“哈哈！那倒是。”一个低沉的声音响起。转眼间一个身影从他右手边的密林里蹿出来，又有一个从左边的树丛中跳出，另一个则在前方好几码外的树干后现身。接着休伯特手中的缰绳便被夺走，自己也被从马上拽下。尽管奋力挣扎，像任何一个英勇的男孩都会做的那样，最终他还是被制服了，双臂捆在身后，两腿紧紧绑在一起。强盗把他扔进道沟后，驾马扬长而去。此时他才勉强看清：那两个人的脸都被故意涂黑了。

当休伯特意识清醒一点时，他发现，虽然自己可以奋力挣脱腿上的绳子，但不管怎么活动，两只胳膊还是捆得严严实实。所以他只能跳起来，双手背在身后前进，希望能够在某一个瞬间把绳结挣开。他知道今晚是走不

到家了，而且还是在这种情况下，但他也没有放弃，依然坚持前进。谁知刚才受到的袭击让脑袋昏昏沉沉的，他很快就迷了路。如果不是很清楚大冬天毫无覆盖地睡在霜地上有多危险，休伯特真想就此躺下，休息一晚。他继续往前走，双臂被绳索绑着拧着，早已麻木，心中想到失去了可怜的杰瑞，便愈加伤痛：他的杰瑞不踹人也不咬人，从没有半点臭毛病。走着走着，休伯特惊喜地看到森林中依稀有微弱的灯光射出。于是他循着光亮向前，最终发现自己来到了一栋有宽阔侧翼、山墙和高塔的大宅前，碉堡之上有城垛和烟囱，映衬在星空下。

四周一片寂静，宅邸的门却赫然洞开，正是门内射出的光吸引他来到这里。进去之后，他发现这个巨大套间是一个餐厅，灯火通明，墙面均铺了深色的护壁板，配有缘饰镶板、各种雕刻、壁橱门柜，以及其他这类大房子里常见的装饰陈设。不过，最吸引休伯特的还是正中央的大桌子，因为上面摆满了珍馐佳肴，是无比丰盛的晚餐，但却未被动过。而桌子四周摆好了餐椅，看起来像是正要开始的晚宴被什么事突然打断了。

就算休伯特再想，他现在这个状况也吃不了，除非把嘴浸在盘子里，像猪牛一样拱着进食，所以当务之急

是看看有没有人能帮忙解开绳子。正当他准备往房子里走时，突然听到门廊处传来匆忙的脚步声和说话声："快点！"这声音低沉，和他从马背上被拖下来时听到的一模一样。他赶紧往桌下一钻，接着三个男人就进来了。休伯特从垂下的桌布边缘偷偷向外望，只见那几个人的脸也是涂黑的，这时他心中最后一点疑问打消了：真是同一伙贼。

"现在，"走在最前的那个人用低沉的嗓音说，"我们快藏起来。他们一会儿就又回来了。这方法不错吧？让他们都出去了。"

"嗯。别说，你模仿惊慌失措的叫声还真挺像。"第二个人说。

"惟妙惟肖。"另一个说。

"不过他们很快就会发现警报是假的，快，我们藏哪儿好呢？最好是能待两三个小时的地方，可以一直等到所有人都上床睡着。啊！知道了。这边！之前听人说过最远的橱柜一年都开不了一次，正合我意。"

说话人出了餐厅进入一条走廊。休伯特悄悄往前爬了些，依稀可以看见伫立在走廊另一头的橱柜，柜门朝着餐厅这边。这几个贼猫腰躲进去，关上了柜门。休伯

特屏住呼吸，向前挪了挪，想要弄清楚他们的意图；凑近后，他听见强盗们在小声谈论哪些房间有金银珠宝，其他值钱的东西藏在哪里，很显然，他们准备行窃。

不一会儿，露台那边开始传来绅士、淑女们的闲谈欢笑声。休伯特意识到如果被人发现自己在房子里鬼鬼祟祟可不太好，除非他想要被当成劫匪给抓起来，于是他悄悄潜回厅外，藏在门廊黑暗的角落里。在这里他可以看见厅内的一切，却不会被人发现。很快，一群人走过来，和休伯特擦身而过，进了房子。其中有一对较为年长的绅士和淑女，还有年轻的小姐和男士各八九位，除此之外随行的男女仆从共有六人。显然，他们才是这栋大房子真正的主人、客人，之前有事出去了。

“孩子们、年轻人，现在，晚宴继续，”老绅士说，“我也不知道刚才的吵闹声是怎么回事，但敢肯定的是，一定有一个人在家门口被杀了。”

随后，女士们开始讨论方才的情形有多么骇人，她们又是怎样暗自期待一场冒险奇遇，结果到头来什么事也没发生。

“等着吧，女士们，”休伯特自言自语道，“不久后你们就会有一场货真价实的冒险了。”

看起来，年轻的男士、女士似乎是老夫妻已婚的儿女们，他们在这一天回家，与父母共度圣诞佳节。

接着大门就关上了，休伯特被留在了门廊外。他意识到这是自己寻求帮助的绝佳时机，由于双手被捆起来了没办法敲，他便开始用身体使劲地撞门。

“喂！在这儿闹什么呢？”开门的男仆质问道，一把抓住休伯特的肩膀，把他拽进餐厅里。“西蒙爵士，我发现这个男孩在门廊里制造噪声，非常可疑。”

所有人都看向休伯特。

“把他带过来。”西蒙男爵说，他正是之前提到的那位老绅士，“孩子，你在那里做什么呀？”

“为什么他的手臂被绑起来了？”其中一位女士说。

“可怜的孩子！”另一位说道。

休伯特立即解释了自己是在回家途中遭受伏击，被盗贼夺去马匹后残忍地抛下，才沦落至此的。

“想想都让人难过！”西蒙爵士大声说道。

“这很可能只是编造的故事。”一位绅士打扮的客人狐疑道。

“你不相信，嗯？”西蒙爵士问。

“也许他自己就是一个盗匪。”一位女士表示。

“我仔细看了他的相貌，长得就邪里邪气，不像好人。”老夫人说道。

休伯特脸唰的一下红了；他没有再说下去，想到强盗们还藏在房子里，他赶紧停住了嘴，一边开始思忖如何让这群人自己发现危险。

“给他松绑吧。”西蒙爵士说，“这样，既然今天是圣诞前夜，我们还是要好好招待一下。来，小伙子，坐在长桌那头的空座上吧，敞开了吃，尽情享用。等你吃饱喝足了，我们再细听你的故事。”

于是盛宴又继续进行着；休伯特现在没有了束缚，一点也不觉得不好意思。他们吃得越多喝得越多，休伯特也就愈加高兴。葡萄酒在人们的杯中芳香四溢，木材燃起熊熊炭火，直顶烟囱，女士们被绅士们讲的故事逗得捧腹大笑；简而言之，周遭一切都是喧闹欢愉的，和那个时候所有热闹的圣诞聚会一样。

人们的欢呼与嬉笑，在座主宾的热闹与狂喜，这场面使休伯特也情不自禁被感染了，虽然因为别人怀疑自己的诚实而有点受伤，但此时他的身心都备感温暖。他渐渐融入其中，到最后，他和老从男爵、西蒙男爵一样，也因为那些风趣故事和妙语如珠而痛快大笑。宴席快结

束的时候，男爵的一个儿子，好像酒喝得多了点，和那个世纪的男人们一样，晃晃悠悠地靠过来跟休伯特说："嘿，我的朋友，最近怎么样啊？要吸撮鼻烟吗？"说着他掏出一个鼻烟盒。这种小盒子当时风靡全国，老人、年轻人都很喜欢。

"谢谢。"休伯特说，吸了一口。

"告诉这些女士们，你是谁，你是做什么的，你能干什么。"年轻男人接着说道，重重拍着休伯特的肩膀。

"当然，"我们的男主人公说，提了提精神，想着最好还是勇敢面对，"我是一个旅行魔术师。"

"没错！"

"接下来要说什么呢？"

"你能从深渊招魂吗，小巫师？"

"我能在橱柜里掀起一场小风暴。"休伯特回答道。

"哈哈！"老从男爵听了兴奋地搓搓手，"那我们可得好好看看。女士们，别走远，好戏就要开始啦。"

"应该不危险吧？"老夫人问。

休伯特从桌旁起身，对刚才那个无礼的年轻人说："请把鼻烟盒递给我一下。""现在，"他继续说道，"请大家保持安静，随我来。任何人出声都会打破咒语。"

于是宾客们都乖乖听话，鸦雀无声。休伯特脱下皮靴，进入走廊，蹑手蹑脚地靠近那扇柜门，其他人默默跟在他后面，保持一小段距离。接着休伯特悄悄在门前放下一只凳子，自己站上去，刚好能够到柜顶。他悄无声息地从上面的柜门外把鼻烟倾倒进去，再呼出短短几口气，就把鼻烟恰好从门缝里吹进了橱柜。他挥手示意人群继续保持安静。

“我的天哪，什么声音？”过了一两分钟后，老夫人说。

只听得柜子里面一声压抑的喷嚏。

休伯特继续示意安静。

“真是奇了怪了，”西蒙爵士小声说，“太有意思了。”

休伯特趁此机会悄悄插紧橱柜的门闩，平静地说：“再来点鼻烟。”

“来点鼻烟。”西蒙爵士说。两三个绅士立即递来几个鼻烟盒，里面的东西继而也从柜门上方被吹了进去。接着又是一声喷嚏，已经不像第一声那样闷了；然后又一声，似乎在诉说自己无论如何都不想压抑了。最后，只听得一阵雷鸣般的喷嚏声此起彼伏。

“非常好，真是年少有为！”西蒙爵士说，“我对这

种发声技巧很感兴趣，我猜，是叫腹语术吧。”

“还需要鼻烟。”休伯特说。

“还需要鼻烟。”西蒙爵士吩咐下去，于是仆从们拿来了一大罐香气浓郁的苏格兰鼻烟。

休伯特再次对准柜门上方的空隙，像之前一样把鼻烟吹进去。反复了好几次，直至把罐子全部清空。喷嚏声变得喧闹起来，毫不费力就能听见——并且一刻不停，就像是暴风雨中狂风、大雨和海水的激荡。

“我想这里面是有人的，根本就不是什么魔术！”西蒙爵士恍然大悟，大声说道。

“是的，”休伯特说，“他们是来打劫的，也是他们抢了我的马。”

此时喷嚏声已转为断断续续的嘟囔呻吟，其中一个贼听到了休伯特的声音，大喊道：“噢！行行好！饶了我吧！让我们出去！”

“我的马在哪儿？”休伯特问。

“系在了山谷间的一棵树上，就在绞刑架后面。行行好！行行好！放我们出去，不然就要被闷死了！”

此时，所有圣诞宾客都明白了，这不是什么消遣戏法，而是严肃的真事。枪和棍棒都已备好，所有男仆也

都被叫进来，严阵以待。信号一发，休伯特抽开门闩，准备好防守姿势。然而这三个强盗哪还有力气攻击他们，早就在柜子角落蜷缩成一团，上气不接下气了。他们毫无抵抗便乖乖束手就擒，绑住双臂后就直接被扔到外屋去，等候明早处置。

休伯特现在才将整个故事向宾客众人娓娓道来，大家都对他的竭力帮助感激不尽。西蒙爵士表示一定要留他下来过夜，并且让他享用大宅子里最好的卧室。伊丽莎白女王和查尔斯王子到访当地时，就曾先后下榻在那间房。不过休伯特婉言谢绝了，因为他迫不及待地要找回自己的小马杰瑞，他要去验证强盗们的说辞是否真实。

几位客人陪着休伯特走到绞刑架后，根据盗贼暗指的意思，杰瑞就藏在这附近。他们走上小圆丘四处查看，瞧！小马就站在那里呢，毫发无伤，而且颇为惬意。一看到休伯特，它便兴奋地嘶叫起来；对于休伯特来说，也没有什么比找到杰瑞更开心了。他骑了上去，向身边朋友们道了声“晚安”，便策马朝着他们所指的方向飞驰，那是回家最近的路。清晨四点前后，他终于平安抵家。

（谢万容　译）

PENGUIN

LITTLE BLACK

CLASSICS

企鹅经典：小黑书　第一辑

01.　贝尔科洛蕾夫人与神父
［意］薄伽丘

02.　泄密的心
［美］爱伦·坡

03.　醋栗
［俄］契诃夫

04.　一个人需要许多土地吗？
［俄］列夫·托尔斯泰

05.　一颗简单的心
［法］福楼拜

06.　傻子的一生
［日］芥川龙之介

07.　萎缩的胳膊
［英］托马斯·哈代

08.　樱花树下的清酒
［日］吉田兼好

09.　虎！虎！
［英］威廉·布莱克

10.　给一个青年诗人的十封信
［奥］里尔克

Penguin Little Black Classics Vol. I

01. GIOVANNI BOCCACCIO
Mrs Rosie and the Priest

02. EDGAR ALLAN POE
The Tell-Tale Heart

03. ANTON CHEKHOV
Gooseberries

04. LEO TOLSTOY
How Much Land Does a Man Need?

05. GUSTAVE FLAUBERT
A Simple Heart

06. RYUNOSUKE AKUTAGAWA
The Life of a Stupid Man

07. THOMAS HARDY
The Withered Arm

08. KENKO
A Cup of Sake Beneath the Cherry Trees

09. WILLIAM BLAKE
Tyger Tyger

10. RAINER MARIA RILKE
Letters to a Young Poet

PENGUIN
LITTLE BLACK
CLASSICS